STUNNER

POWERHOUSE INSTITUTE 1

ATHENA FRANCO

1 LULLABY

From: Dr. Sara Singh
    <singhsarafac@powerallinstitute.mail>
To: Briar Williams
<williamsbriarstu@powerallinstitute.mail>
Subject: Your Internship

Hi Briar,

I have some urgent news about your pending internship. Can you stop by my office today?

Sara Singh, PhD | Research Associate, Professor
    Department of Preternatural Psychologies
    Powerall Institute

.   .   .

Urgent.

The word echoed in my head as I watched the red numbers above the doors change. The elevator hummed as it carried me and one other person up the floors.

Seeing as he was unconscious, I didn't bother exchanging small talk.

He sprawled at my feet, collapsed atop the backpack he'd left sitting in the middle of the floor. The bag that caused me to trip in the first place.

I'd stumbled, the sudden shock making my powers flare to life. It churned under my skin, ready to defend me. I flailed and the guy reached out to catch me.

One touch was all it took. His hands caught hold of my bare arms and down he went, my ability plunging him deep into sleep.

I bit my lip, wiped my damp palms against my dress slacks. My uncle's voice rang through my head. Warning me that I'd let my guard down, messed up my only chance at superhero success.

"This is your one shot, Briar. You won't get another one. Don't screw it up."

I shoved the voice out of my head, tried to think of a solution. But what the hell was I supposed to do? Throw a table cloth and a potted plant on him? Tape a sign to his chest, "Sleep protest in progress, do not disturb?"

The elevator pinged open. I held my breath, a half-assed explanation on my lips.

The corridor stood empty.

I exhaled, pulse racing. Though guilt churned in my stomach, I couldn't hang around waiting for Sleepy to rise and shine. He'd wake up soon, no worse for wear. Meanwhile my internship, my future, was riding on this meeting.

I shoved my foot in front of the elevator door, my other

hand rooting around in my bag until I found a pen and a scrap of paper. Still trying to keep the doors open, I managed to scrawl my name, contact code, and "Sorry!" in big letters.

I tucked the note under one of his backpack straps then rushed out of the elevator, down the corridor into the faculty wing.

The glass doors slid open as I approached, the cool air washing over me. I passed through the open lobby, the wide space arranged with white coffee tables and sleek waiting chairs.

A holoscreen flared to life, emitting a calm, soothing voice. "Welcome to Powerall Institute's faculty offices. How may I assist you today?"

The screen went back into sleep mode as I passed through it. It was late midmorning, and everyone was scrambling to get work done before the lunch rush. Faculty members and student assistants darted around or tapped furiously at holoscreens. The offices smelled of clean circulated air, brewed coffee, and someone's toasted bagel.

A young woman with deep brown skin marched down the hall, half a dozen cups of to go coffee trailing in the air behind her like balloons. A blur of movement passed in the corner of my eye as someone teleported from one spot to another. He paused long enough for me to catch a glimpse of warm brown skin and black hair before he was gone again.

I gripped the straps of my shoulder bag. Both the teleporter and the telekinetic were my age, and likely candidates for professional licensure. Side hustles sometimes made all the difference at the institute.

Another assistant rushed by, her blazer a deep green against bronze skin, her thick brown hair in a bun.

She paused to greet me. "Hey, Briar."

"Ashley." I smiled back. Ashley was a latent, but that hadn't stopped her from earning a coveted position as one of Dr. Singh's research assistants.

"Want some black tea?"

"I'm good." I had too much energy as it was.

That's my ability, energy transference. Depending on how much I drew, it could make the other person fatigued, exhausted, or knock them right out.

Now, Elevator Guy's energy coiled through me. It was like I'd taken a shot of caffeine, my heartbeat rapid, my senses on high alert.

Elevator Guy, on the other hand, was going to wake up groggy, confused, and pissed. I burned his appearance into my brain to remember him. Asian-American features, slashing dark brows. Thick black hair, a strong, masculine face. Good looking. A lean, muscled body, pale gold skin.

Thinking about him made my stomach twist. I had decent control over my powers. I was in superhero grad school, after all. But any PN can suffer from occasional spikes and mishaps. If our bodies or minds think we're in danger, our abilities lash out. Being tired or angry made it more likely.

Or, in my case, stressed.

I said goodbye to Ashley, rapped on my advisor's door.

"Come in."

I pushed through the door into Dr. Singh's tidy office. A gleaming white desk filled most of the space, the surface arranged with matching black and white office supplies. Certificates and awards hung on the wall behind her. Framed photographs of her with accomplished graduates occupied another wall.

Trailing ivy plants flourished near the windows, pouring over the sides of beaten copper pots. They kicked out a watery, green smell that mixed with the scent of her black tea. A wallscreen played the news on mute.

Dr. Singh looked up from her screen. "Briar. You're right on time." Her black hair hung in a neat twist over one shoulder, her suit a vibrant violet against her warm brown skin.

I put on a smile that I hoped projected calm confidence. "Thank you for meeting with me."

"Please have a seat."

I pinned a smile to my face and sat down, ready to wow her with my can-do attitude.

"I'm afraid your internship has been cancelled."

2 LULLABY

My smile turned to a shocked gape. "What?"

"I'm afraid so." Her finger skimmed over the screen, bringing up a document. "Here."

My hands shook as I tapped at the mini HC on my wrist. The little holocomputer was about an inch by inch. A standard model. Mine was nestled in a pretty bracelet made of rose quartz stones. A gift from my dad for getting into the institute.

The tiny light gleamed as it projected a palm-sized screen in the air in front of me. Messages popped up, including one from my uncle. I quickly dismissed them, expanded the window.

Dr. Singh flicked the document on her screen, causing it to appear on mine. I accepted the sent file and opened it, my brow furrowing as I read the text. "'The position is no longer available.'"

"It's unfortunate when these things happen." Dr. Singh laced her fingers together. "The real question is, what do we do now?"

Panic, I thought.

I pressed my lips together. Four years of advanced courses in high school, two in state college. If I counted my freshman year at the institute, they added up to seven of busting my ass. Juggling work, classes, assignments. Endless counseling sessions and private tutors and cram courses to overcome my "weak areas."

And Powerall's had a strict time cap for earning a license. Second chances were practically nonexistent. The institute was too competitive to leave room for failures.

I swallowed, fought to get my nerves under control. "Should I make an appointment with the career counselor?"

"I think," said Dr. Singh. "We're past the point where additional counseling would be helpful."

This was it. They were kicking me out.

The back of my throat burned. In the time I'd spent there, the institute had become my home. I had friends who'd become family, co-workers, professors who cared. And now I was going to walk away, a complete failure. Just as my uncle had predicted.

Dr. Singh's words cut through my racing thoughts. "Instead, I want to recommend you to our Paired Independent Study Program. It's brand new, and I'm hoping we'll be able to offer it to candidates who have those degree gaps. Especially those with potential."

"Don't look so surprised," she went on when I hesitated. "You've had some, shall we say, adjustment issues. However, your attitude is excellent and your commitment to your degree is exemplary."

"Thank you," I said, mentally pumping my fist. Those weekends and holiday breaks spent doing extra credit work and having zero social life were finally paying off! "What's the program?"

"It's something I've been developing on the side." She

leaned forward, her features lighting up. "You'll be participating in the trial run. Depending on how well it goes, I'll be presenting it as possible alternative curriculum to the board."

Right away, I understood. This was an initiative she was spearheading. This project was her baby. No surprise she was pushing for it. The professors at Powerall's were as competitive as the students.

"At its core, the program emphasizes working alongside someone else for its duration," she said. "You and your assigned partner will work in tandem, figuring out how to best synergize your separate strengths, and present a thesis on your work. It's excellent preparation for post-graduate life."

It was true, most licensed "preternaturals," as scientists called us, worked in pairs or teams. It was safer for everyone involved, and the stronger your partnership, the better chance of getting the assignments you wanted.

My heart sped up. This was it. My one chance to make sure the last seven years didn't go to waste.

Plus seeing the enthusiasm on Dr. Singh's face made me want to be a part of it. She'd done so much for me over the years. Recommending trainers, encouraging me when I flagged. It was probably my superhero nature kicking in, but I wanted to help her if I could.

"Depending on how this trial goes," she continued. "We'll use the results to improve the parameters. You'll be part of something that will have a long lasting impact on Powerall's."

No pressure. Still, I found myself leaning forward. "Sounds great."

Even as I said it, part of me balked at the idea of working in a team. There was always someone who cruised along, riding everyone else's efforts. Or someone who was never satisfied, dragging the process. Things got even more complicated between PNs. We had a tendency to be competitive, wanting to one up each other.

Dr. Singh flicked through her screen. "I'll send you the info packet, it outlines the details. We'll go over it more closely once you've met your partner."

"You have someone in mind?"

"Like you, he has enough gaps in credits to make it a worthwhile endeavor. He's on a different specialization track than you are, which is ideal. We want the program to assist the separate branches in understanding and communicating with one another."

Made sense. Abilities among PNs spanned a wide range, from the small and simple to the extraordinary. We could work in a lot of diverse fields. Chasing down purse snatchers to battling intergalactic invaders.

All of which required a license from an accredited training facility. There were only two in the U.S., both with wait lists stretching to infinity. The requirements for entry and graduation were cutthroat.

I fisted my hands in my lap. I'd fought long and hard to get in and then stay at the institute. Sacrificed what little free time I'd had as a teen to beef up my resume, add to my recommendations, apply for every scholarship. I had to do everything possible to make this trial a success.

Footsteps behind me drew my attention. I turned, plastering a smile on my face.

For the second time, my smile turned into a gape.

"Ah, here he is. Briar, this is Jase Park. Jase, this is Briar."

I gripped the chair handles, my lungs locked as I stared at the man in the doorway. The very gorgeous man.

The one I'd left asleep in the elevator.

3   STRONGHOLD

I've woken up in weird places before. Bathtubs, basements. Battlefields.

Elevator? New one.

"Is he alright?"

"Is he dead?"

I snapped awake, lurching to a sitting position. The two young women leaning over me startled. One of them was carrying a to go coffee. She gasped, dropping her cup.

Scalding hot liquid sloshed over my shoulders, down my chest. It soaked into my clothes, steaming off my skin.

"Oh my God! We'll take you to the clinic!"

"Cold water," said the other. "You need to rinse burns."

"I'm alright." I stood, tapped my chest. "Invincibility."

The two of them exhaled sighs of relief.

A little cleaning robot wandered over, asked us to mind our step as it whirred over the mess. A soggy slip of paper fell from my bag, hit the floor in a sodden lump before the robot gobbled it up.

I glanced at my HC, grimaced. I needed to get a move on.

I grabbed the back of my shirt, pulled it off over my head. The two women stared as I traded it for a clean one from my backpack.

The woman who'd dropped the coffee put a hand to her chest. "Wow, you're..."

"Invincible." I tugged the shirt over my torso, confused when they continued to linger. "I'm fine. Sorry about your coffee."

"Perhaps we can get some together. My treat."

"I'm good, thanks." I turned, headed for the stairs.

As I climbed, I thought over what happened. I'd set my bag down to answer a signal on my HC. I didn't notice the woman who'd entered the elevator until I was reaching out to catch her mid fall.

For a second, she'd been in my arms, her full pink lips parting. Sky blue eyes, pale skin, a scatter of freckles. Hair the color of sunshine. A lush body with soft curves. A stunner.

I'd caught a whiff of vanilla as everything went black.

I ground my teeth. She must've used her ability on me, left me like road kill.

Now I was late.

I picked up the pace until I reached the right floor. The door opened to the low hum of the faculty wing. People closed screens, hauled bags onto shoulders, eager to escape the offices for lunch.

A blur and rush of air beside me. It swirled and turned solid, revealing a Hispanic American guy with brown skin and black hair.

"Hey, man."

"Hector." We knocked fists. The two of us worked together freshman year on a few assignments. Since then, we met up either for training or video games, depending on who was doing the choosing.

"Want to hit Bruce's tomorrow? They probably serve those shakes you live off of."

"Milk shakes and nutrient shakes aren't the same thing."

"True, one's way better tasting. Powerhouses can't live on simulated proteins alone. I'll ping you." He was gone before I could refuse, vanishing in a swirl of air and light.

I hurried on to the office, rapped on the already open door. My shoulders tensed as I locked eyes with Dr. Singh's other guest.

The stunner from the elevator.

"Ah, here he is. Briar, this is Jase Park. Jase, Briar Williams. She'll be your partner for the Paired Independent Study Program."

Of fucking course.

I settled in the empty chair, studied her out of the corner of my eye. Her posture was stiff, her lips pressed together. She wore a trim white button shirt and grey slacks. Interview wear.

Dr. Singh beamed. "For the duration of the project, the two of you will be partners. Allies. Teammates."

No chance in hell. Partners implied cooperation. Trust.

"You each have the right number of credits, you're in different specialties, and I'm an advisor for both of you." Dr. Singh's voice grew animated. "I'll be able to oversee your work."

"If I decline?" I asked. Next to me, Briar grimaced.

"Well, I suppose we'd try to find another candidate. The problem is I pushed to get the program running this semester. The institute's roster of special programs is filled for the next millennium. We might not get another chance. Plus there's the cut off date for add/drop."

Briar's expression tightened, her hands clutched in her lap. "Could we talk it over?"

"Of course. Why don't the two of you discuss and let me know your decision by Monday."

"So soon?" asked Briar.

"The program is still in its experimental stage. If we don't get moving, you won't have time to get it approved ahead of the cut off." Dr. Singh rose, grabbed her bag. "Now, I've got a lunch date."

She left, hurrying towards the elevators. Briar and I exited her office. The faculty wing was quiet, most people having gone to lunch.

Briar kept pace with me until we reached the elevators. Before I could speak, she said, "I'm sorry. For abandoning you like that. I didn't want to be late, but that's no excuse."

I paused, trying to decide if she meant it. She shifted in place, turning her bracelet around her wrist, her brow furrowed and her bottom lip between her teeth.

"I got it," I said.

"Great." She gave a short laugh. "Would've been really awkward as partners."

The elevator opened. I held the door as Briar entered first. "I'm turning down the project."

She frowned, back straightening. "You wouldn't be nominated unless you needed it. Like me."

She wasn't wrong. Every success, every positive review, was another notch in my favor. Not everyone was going to overlook my past the way Dr. Singh did.

But I wasn't going to risk my future on another person. Too much room for error. Too many chances for someone to screw you over.

"Can't we at least talk it over?" Briar stared up at me through long black lashes. She caught that full bottom lip between her teeth.

Dammit.

"I'm busy until four tomorrow," I heard myself say.

She smiled, lighting up. "Coffee? My treat."

Second time a woman had offered to treat me to coffee within an hour. Weird. "Sure. But we'll split it. I already accepted your apology."

"Fair enough. Jubilee's?"

"Works."

We tapped our HCs, exchanged contact info. "Thanks again, Jase. And—"

"No more apologies. Deal?"

"Yes. Er, deal." She extended her hand, flinched, started to pull it back.

I reached out, took her hand. Held until the doors opened to the lobby.

I exited after she did, headed towards the building's parking lot. Tried to forget the way I'd given in to a pretty face.

4 LULLABY

I stood in front of the building, trying to get a grip on myself. Jase accepted my apology, but he'd obviously been wary of me.

I didn't blame him, but I could tell I wasn't going to get many chances to convince him. I needed to make the most of our meeting. Prove the project was worth it.

I followed the pathway winding down the main street. Powerall Institute sprawled hundreds of acres, lots of rolling lawns and winding walkways. The nearly ever-present Florida sun beamed, warming the late summer air. Quintessential palm trees waved in the gentle breeze, though there enough oak and pine trees to remind me of home.

The buildings were a mix of the old Spanish style, gleaming white walls and red tiled roofs, and ultra modern glass and steel. A blend of laid back Florida vibes and hyper-advanced technology.

People lounged on benches, slept in the shade, strolled the stone walkways. A horse galloped over the lawns, a backpack clenched between its teeth. Two teleporters played frisbee, each disappearing and reappearing in random locations. A leaping figure bounded across rooftops in giant, gravity-defying arcs.

I slothed my way through my afternoon Ethics and Leadership for PNs class and then headed for my work shift at the on-campus resource center. The tall windows spilled ample sunshine into the main space. Round tables and chairs ranged in rows, offering access to charging stations.

A handful of students swiped and tapped at open use HCs. An older woman, probably a professor, sat scowling and tapping a stylus against a screen. The atmosphere was quiet except for finger swipes and the occasional shuffle of a chair.

I spent the next few hours doing everything from tutoring to helping file applications. My job looked good on resumes, but I genuinely liked mentoring.

"It's your voice," said Victoria.

I stood in front of the vending machine, weighing my options. "What about it?"

The two of us were in the resource center's tiny employee break room. Small tables lined the walls, each flanked by metal chairs. A screen played the news on low volume. The smell of old coffee and reheated pasta filled the air.

Victoria lounged in a chair, her screen open and dimmed in front of her. Through it, I could see her big brown eyes and gold skin. Her black jacket and skinny jeans molded to her hourglass frame, her wavy brown hair hanging in an intricate braid.

"It's soothing or something. Like a fountain or crashing waves."

"Have you been writing bad poetry again?"

She made a face. "The point is, you're easy to talk to."

I was a highly requested tutor. I'd thought it was my innate, if boring, talent of filling out forms. Nice to know I was good at helping others.

I settled on a safe bet, jabbed the button. A bottle of Rocket Water, lemon-mint flavor, hit the bin with a dull clunk.

I sat and sipped, pairing the water with a granola bar. Since it was formulated for PNs, the label read, "Now with 10x the calories!"

"If that's true," I said. "Why doesn't everyone obey me?"

"They will if you say the right thing."

"Super helpful."

"I mean it. You've got a trustworthy face. Anyone would listen."

She went back to the front desk, leaving me alone in the break room.

I pulled up a screen to Jase's contact info. His image appeared, along with an autolink to his student profile page.

I skimmed it. Sky high grades, a dizzying number of certificates. Advanced combat, marathon running, martial arts. Bouldering.

No wonder Dr. Singh chose him. A background like his would impress any approval board.

I read on. Though most of us didn't hide our identities, we still used call signs for any official work.

"Stronghold." The name suited him. The steady gaze in his dark eyes, the strong cut to his jaw. He'd been guarded during the meeting. On edge the entire time.

Would he be like that as a partner? The thought was exhausting.

I searched for his Impulse feed, hoping to find interests. Music and movies made for easy conversation starters.

But in contrast to the official profile, his Impulse feed was barren. No updates, no images or videos.

Considering everyone shared their lives on Impulse, Jase's

lack of online info left a lot of questions. Why the mystery? Was he a spy? Witness protection?

A notification popped up. I grimaced, accepted the call. "Hi, Uncle Brian."

He ran a hand over his hair. Like me, he was blonde, blue eyed, lightly freckled. "How are classes?"

"Fine."

"I'm concerned. You struggled your first year."

My stomach tightened, the water tasting bitter in my mouth.

This was the real reason I avoided his calls. Not only did he try to micromanage me, he used my previous mistakes as a hammer. In the ten years since my father and I moved in with him, he hadn't let one thing slip. Coming home late, getting a B on a test, winning second place. All more than enough to earn the Uncle Brian stamp of disapproval.

Patience, I reminded myself. Once I graduated, I could work as a licensed PN in any number of fields. I could buy my dad a house with a garden and a real library stuffed with the physical books he cherished.

"I have to get back to work." I said a quick goodbye, closed the screen, and let my forehead hit the table.

It was getting harder and harder to be civil. Especially now. Living at the institute gave me a taste of what life was like without his constant scrutiny.

Victoria poked her head around the door. "Hey, Hawthorne called. You okay?"

I plastered on a smile. "What did the boss say?"

"We've got a slew of freshmen coming in for a tour."

I pulled together, headed for the front desk.

A few more years, I reminded myself. Which meant acing the partner program. Uncle Brian's call had reminded me what was at stake. Freedom for me and my dad.

I just had to convince a guy who hated me that we'd be perfect as partners.

5 STRONGHOLD

Air rushed over my skin as I pounded down the track, keeping to the center of my lane. I controlled my breathing, timing it with the fast pace I was keeping. My focus stayed on the course, watching for any sudden movements.

Behind me, the track was a wreck of broken combat dummies and destroyed obstacles. Busted swing bags hung limp, spilling their contents. The stench of scorched ozone filled the air, the only sound my measured breaths.

I put on speed, arms pumping. A jump shot up from the ground, right in front of me. I planted a hand on the surface, swung myself over.

A shock dummy leaped. I braced and barreled into it, gritting my teeth at the mild electric jolt it delivered. Invulnerability protected me against physical damage until the well ran dry, but wasn't as effective against things like electricity. The longer I came into contact with it, the more damage I'd take.

I grabbed the dummy by the base and wrenched it in half. The metal squealed as it twisted apart. The dummy wheezed and twitched as it died. The lights on its surface changed from red to green, signaling I'd cleared the obstacle.

I surged past the checkpoint, reducing my speed to a jog. My HC popped up a screen, offering me records on my performance. Time per obstacle, variation of technique.

My jaw tightened as I studied the numbers. Not bad, not great. I could do better.

While I toweled off, the track reset. The holographic obstacles faded, the projectors readying for the next round. The computer reminded me my session was almost over.

The recreation building housed typical campus facilities. Gyms, pools, basketball courts. I spent most of my time in the holographic training tracks. They kept my reflexes sharp and supplemented my usual workouts.

Grabbing my bag, I left the HTT, cut across to the indoor gyms. Bright white lights illuminated the wide space. Screens opened near each station, offering entertainment choices. A cleaning robot wandered, spritzing surfaces with a lemon scented disinfectant.

People huffed and grunted through workouts. Weights clanked, treadmills whirred. Behind glass walls, a sparring class took place, the instructor urging on participants.

Knowing how to fight was crucial. There were always criminals to fight. Common emergencies were more likely, though. Search and rescue, disaster relief, humanitarian aid. All of it meant being in top physical and mental health.

I put in the hours, kept myself in peak condition. When the time came, I wanted to prove I could handle anything thrown at me.

My HC chimed.

Incoming Video Call: Sis

. . .

Leaving the gym, I searched the lobby for a quiet corner and an empty bench.

The screen opened, revealing my sister's face. "Hey, baby bro. How's the super life?"

I smiled. We'd had pretty different upbringings. Though we'd both come from PN parents, Cassi hadn't manifested any abilities. Only about 5% of the population were PNs. Even fewer were latent.

Latency hadn't held her back. Whether it was her career, her social life, or being a nosy big sister, she went full throttle.

I dug a bottle of Rocket Water out of my bag. "What's up?"

"Just making sure you're coming next weekend."

"Wouldn't miss it."

"Great! I'm excited. The club looks amazing. Also, it's kind of a dating event."

My grip on the bottle tightened. "Forget it."

"Come on, Jase. Couples events are the big trend right now. Besides, it'll be good for you."

"Like last time?"

"How was I supposed to know she was a groupie?"

"Groupie" was putting it mildly. The woman had shown up wearing a t-shirt reading, "I <3 Soopies!" and immediately asked me to film a video with her for her Impulse.

"I'm not boyfriend material," I said.

"Untrue! And don't give me the 'I want to focus on my career' excuse."

I grimaced. This was the fifth time my sister had tried to set me up. It never went well.

I got it. She was in a longterm, blissful relationship. She was in love, and it made her so happy she'd decided it was what everyone needed. Since then, she'd declared it her side project to get me a girlfriend.

I was happy for her and Alba, but these dates were a waste of time. Time better spent training and studying.

"Why the rush to pair me off?" I asked.

"Because I know you. You're holing up at superhero school, working day and night. I bet you haven't left campus in weeks."

"Been busy."

"You should be having fun, seeing friends. Bringing girlfriends home so I can reveal embarrassing childhood stories."

"Can't imagine why I'm dragging my feet."

She laughed, then sobered. "Lydia did a number on us. You can't let what happened hold you back from potential happiness."

I set my jaw, my shoulders tightening. "Right."

"It's settled. I'll set you up with a nice girl. Unless you have someone in mind."

"I don't."

"Great. See you then!"

Great.

Part of me wanted to turn her down. I had other priorities. But it was damn hard for me to refuse anything that made Cassi happy.

By the time I showered, my HC was reminding me to meet Briar for coffee. I grabbed my gear and caught the next skyrail.

A smaller, more compact version of the city system, the sleek, narrow cabs cruised high above the ground, guided by a network of invisible mag-levs. Riders chatted, stared at screens. Holoscreens near the ceiling alternated between on-campus news and calendars with upcoming events.

I shifted, making room as the doors opened. The young

woman beside me bumped my side. Her palm slapped against my chest.

"Hey, watch—" She stopped. Her frown turned to a smile. "Oh, sorry. My fault."

"No problem." I waited for her to move away.

Waited.

The guy with her growled. "Hands off, buddy."

"Don't be fault, Eric." The woman rolled her eyes.

Fire erupted, wrapping around his fists in flaming gloves. "He touched you, Chris. I saw it."

Chris glared. Electricity sparked and snapped along her skin, her hair billowing into a cloud from the static. "For the last time, knock it off."

"But, baby!"

Flames and sparks snapped in the air around them. Onlookers glanced over before shifting to give them more room. Overhead, the intercom speakers reminded us to please watch our footing due to recent construction.

The train pulled into the station. I got off, even though I had several stops to go. I drew in a long breath, shouldered my bag, and started walking.

Between elevators and trains, it seemed it was a good week for going on foot.

6 LULLABY

L   ULLABY: Still on for coffee?
        STRONGHOLD: Yes.
LULLABY: Great! See you then!
STRONGHOLD: Yes.

"Don't scowl." Victoria nudged me with her elbow. "You're scaring the freshmen."

I fixed my face, closed the screen. Not sure what I expected, but my stoic exchange with Jase was discouraging.

It was the day of our meeting to discuss the project. I'd poured over Dr. Singh's info packet, highlighted relevant portions, made notes.

At first, I'd done it to prepare for my meeting with Jase. But I found myself involved and engaged. I could see the potential in the project, and read Dr. Singh's passion in the words.

I left work and headed for Jubilee's. It was a typical gorgeous afternoon, all warm weather and balmy breezes. Though my hometown was only a two hour drive north,

Mayport felt worlds away from where I'd grown up. The high percentage of PNs living and working there, the diverse population, the fast-paced energy.

I spotted Jase near the entrance, gaze fixed on his HC screen. A young woman with tanned skin and sand-blonde hair was attempting to make conversation with him, an iced drink dangling from her fingertips. Her eyelashes were fluttering a mile a minute, her head tilted.

Couldn't blame her. He was tall and sculpted, shoulders tapering to his waist in a way that had me imagining running my hand over his chest, down his stomach.

Jase listened, pointed down the street, said two words, went back to his screen. The woman tossed her hair, tried again. Jase's brow furrowed as he listened, expression puzzled.

I wasn't sure whether to feel sorry for him or for the woman.

I stepped up, cleared my throat. "Sorry I'm late."

Jase frowned as the woman stormed off. "What's with her?"

"Oblivious boys." At his arched brow, I laughed, my mood lifted. After dealing with classes, work, and my uncle, it felt good. "It's the name of my next band."

"You play music?"

Oh boy. "Never mind."

Jase held the door for me as we entered. The rich aroma of brewed coffee and sweet baked goods hit me, a wall of deliciousness. I breathed deep. Coffee shop smell was among my favorite smells.

Faint music piped over the speakers, something acoustic and indie. Dark wood tables and chairs spanned the room, lined the walls. Student art hung in frames, ranging from moody photographs to abstract postmodern.

Rows of cold cases lined one wall, offering snacks and bottled drinks. A short woman with brown skin and natural, curly hair stood in front of the chips, trying to reach a bag on the highest shelf.

Behind the counter, an enormous vintage espresso machine filled the back wall. Twisting arms and knobs made it look like a steampunk monster, the brass surface gleamed under the warm ceiling lights. It whirred and groaned as the baristas buzzed around it. Pipes hissed, steam billowed. A barista snapped his fingers over orders as he made them, causing them to disappear from in front of him and reappear on the pick-up counter.

I turned to tell Jase something only to find him walking off. He approached the woman at the chip display.

"Regular?" he asked.

The woman blinked, her eyes widening as she drank him in. "Barbecue." Her smile turned flirty as he passed her the chips. "Thanks."

He gave her a curt nod and turned away, not noticing her look of disappointment.

The guy was seriously clueless. It was adorable.

"Snacks on me." I tapped my HC to the pay pad. "I insist."

"In that case."

I grinned, ordered a mini dulce de leche cupcake and an iced caramel mocha piled with whipped cream.

Jase flicked through the menu, made his selections. Green tea, an apple, and a packet of low sodium roasted almonds.

The partnership was doomed before it even started.

We snagged our trays and scouted out a table near the windows. The wooden chairs scraped against the tile floors as we sat. Customers crowded the tables, talking or swiping at screens while sipping from the shop's signature yellow cups. A pale, redheaded guy slouched near the sugar station, yawning and stretching. In front of him, packets of sugar tore themselves open and dumped their contents into his cup before tossing themselves into the recomposter.

I took a long sip, the combination of caffeine, chocolate, and caramel bolstering me. Go in positive and strong, I thought.

"So," I began.

"I don't want a partner."

Great start.

"You haven't heard me out."

"I work better alone."

"Lone wolf type, huh?"

To my surprise, Jase's mouth curved. He gave a low, rough chuckle.

My pulse kicked. Was that a flash of dimple?

"What type are you?" he asked.

"The type who wants to earn her license." Desperately.

"You don't want to be saddled with me for a whole semester."

My heart sank. Maybe finding alternatives would work for Mr. High Achiever, but I had no doubts where I'd end up.

Student purgatory. The wait list for extending the attendance cap was even longer than the one for entry. Most of the people on it had far more impressive backgrounds than mine. Re-entry could take years. If it happened at all.

I pictured having to tell my dad. He wouldn't love me any less, would tell me to find my own happiness rather than worry about him. But the idea of him knowing I'd failed left my stomach raw.

I leaned forward. "If Dr. Singh recommended you for the program, you're in need of some extra help, too."

His expression flattened. "Your point?"

Oops, maybe that was the wrong thing to say.

I grasped for a way to keep him listening. Dr. Singh and the approval board were more likely to see the project as a success if their top choices participated. I wanted to convince Jase to give it a chance. To give me a chance.

"We'll be helping each other. Dr. Singh even gave us a list of potential topics to get us started. We get through the program, make it a success for Dr. Singh. Win win." I hoped I sounded more confident than I felt.

He studied me for a long moment. "I'll think about it."

I deflated. He might as well have said, "I don't want to tell you no to your face, I'll wait a few hours and then message it instead."

I'd made my case and failed.

Jase grabbed my tray as we stood. Our fingers brushed, his warm and rough. I remembered the grip of his hands when he'd caught me. Firm, supportive. Gentle.

"Briar."

The way he spoke my name, voice low and a little raspy, sent a thrill through me. This close, I could study the strong line of his jaw, the outline of his lips.

"I'll consider it." He met my gaze, held. "Promise."

My HC pinged, flashed red. "Damn, a signal."

"Need a ride?"

7 LULLABY

I started to refuse him, then paused. The traffic this time of day was a nightmare. Even with the city's efficient public transportation systems, it would take me awhile to get there.

And this was a signal. The sooner I responded, the better. "Okay. Thanks."

We left the coffee shop and headed for the parking lot. "Ace, rendezvous," Jase said. His HC chirped in reply.

A second later, a sleek grey vehicle pulled up to the curb. The sides and window seems were completely smooth, so shiny I could clearly see my reflection.

I stared as a panel slid to one side in front of me. Blue lighting along the creases flared, revealing the black interior. The seats were smooth leather with cushy buckets.

"I don't recognize the model."

"She's not on the market."

Whoa. Was Jase a rich boy? Or maybe the son of a tech empire?

I climbed into the passenger seat, breathing in the smell of clean car. The door panel slid closed and a pleasant voice reminded me to fasten my safety belt.

The dash lit up the moment our belts were locked in, projecting several holoscreens into the air in front of Jase. More appeared before me, offering entertainment choices and displaying time, weather, and a map.

"Where to?" he asked.

"Mayport General."

The vehicle chirped as it it confirmed our destination, gliding away from the curb. I didn't realize we were moving until I saw traffic whizzing by.

"This thing's beyond." I peered out the windows. We were already veering off campus without the lurch or pull of turns. If I didn't watch the world going by, I'd assume we were stopped. "Does it play music?"

Jase flicked one of the screens. It shifted in the air, coming to rest in front of me. "Go ahead." He swiped at a screen, pulling up what looked like notes from a class. An advanced mathematics class, if I interpreted the signs and squiggles correctly.

I flicked through the options on the music menu. "What's your favorite AlterEgo song?"

"Who?"

Partnership, doomed.

"Earbuds on the dash," he said.

Leaving the music for the moment, I dug around for the compression packet I kept in my bag. It was the size of my palm, and heavy. "Mind if I change?"

He swiped at a screen. The windows went black, blocking anyone from seeing in.

I unzipped the packet and the bodysuit spilled out. I glanced at Jase. "No peeking."

He held up his hands, palms out.

My cheeks burned as I started to undress. We were supposed to wear our uniforms whenever we did any official PN work. It kept things professional, helped civilians recognize us.

Many PNs wore theirs under their clothing at all times, but it looked weird wearing a full bodysuit under dresses or skirts. Which meant I got used to changing in cars, public restrooms, wherever.

I'd changed in a bush once. Not fun.

Still, disrobing in such a narrow space with a guy right there made me feel exposed. I turned my back to him as much as possible.

I twisted and tugged my way into the bodysuit. The suits were customized to the wearer, a long process of countless fittings and trials. Whatever they used to make these things was some high tech stuff. In addition to being fire-proof, blade-resistant, and laser resistant, they came in lots of colors. They were durable, form-fitting, supportive.

They had to be. When fighting criminals, a gal needed something that's not going to cause wardrobe malfunctions.

I gathered my hair into a ponytail, slapped my hospital issued ID to my belt. "You can look. Unless you have been this whole time."

I was teasing, but I caught the red flush on Jase's face. Maybe he wasn't as impervious to my charms as I'd assumed.

He glanced at the crest on my arm. "What's that?"

I put my teeth together and buzzed through them.

"Come again?"

"'Zzz.' You know, the sound of someone sleeping?"

Jase's lips twitched. "Okay."

I smiled. "I've been thinking of changing it. Have you ever changed yours?"

"Once." His expression cooled.

Longest conversation we'd had so far. I decided to count it as a victory.

We cruised towards the center of the city. The roads became wide, multi-lane streets with complicated intersections. The sidewalks contained the human version of traffic, and endless flow of pedestrians. A skyrail cruised overhead, casting us in shadow for a moment.

The car eased in and out of lanes. The automated systems steered us through the lightest portions of traffic, gliding in and out of side streets I hadn't even known existed.

Even knowing everything was automated, I held my breath when we came within an inch of another vehicle. "Easy, Ace."

The car beeped. "Please let me know what I can do to make your ride more comfortable."

"Just watch where you're going, speedy."

A low laugh. I glanced over.

Jase was smiling, his dark eyes full of amusement. There was definitely a dimple.

"Relax," he said. "You're safe."

Hard to do when the sight of that dimple had me worked up. Dimples were definitely cheating.

He reached over, covered my hand with his. I realized I'd been gripping the handle on the side of the seat.

I let go and he moved his hand. Too bad. The contact felt nice.

We got to the hospital in half the time it would've taken me to get there by rail. The immense glass and metal building gleamed white in the sun, the hospital name in bold blue and white lettering. An ambulance pulled out as we neared the drop off point, sirens howling.

"Call if you need a ride home," he said as I climbed out. "I'll come get you."

The offer warmed me. "Thanks for the lift." The car pulled away as I turned to enter the hospital.

A cluster of doctors and nurses waited for me in the lobby. My boots clicked against the linoleum as we walked down the corridor.

"Details?" I asked.

A handsome black man wearing a doctor's jacket kept pace next to me. He consulted his screen. "Nine year old, female, non-PN. Her system is weak from being in and out of surgery, but she needs more procedures."

I followed them to the room where the patient waited. A little girl lay on the bed, looking small. Defenseless. Tubes stretched from her to various machines.

Two men stood near the bed, clasping hands. They raced over when they saw me. "Please. Our daughter. She needs this surgery."

Superhero 101. Don't promise, do reassure. "What's her name?"

"Lizzie. Elizabeth."

"I'm going to do everything I can for Lizzie."

The doctor who'd escorted me turned from checking the readouts. "We're ready."

I took a breath, gathered myself. Even though she was sedated, I spoke to her, kept my voice soothing. "Hi, Lizzie. I'm Briar. Is it okay if I take your hand?"

I rested my hand on top of hers and tapped into the well of power deep within me.

My ability responded, awakening under my skin. My powers allowed me to draw energy from others and into my body. I could also reverse the flow, give my energy to others. Kind of like a blood transfusion.

Until I'd come to the institute, I hadn't realized the extent

of my abilities. Now, I was on call with the city's largest
hospital, ready to support any patient who needed me.

Once I earned my license, I'd be part of the Safety Net, a
global system of licensed PNs. I could respond to emergencies,
be on site to keep people alive until doctors could go to work,
act as support squad for other PNs.

It was one of my biggest goals in life. To help. To save.

My powers reached out, searching for the girl's life force. It
lay buried deep inside her, a tiny trickle. I opened the stream of
my energy, guided it through our joined hands. Like an IV drip,
I had to control the amount I gave her. Too much would
overwhelm her. Too little would have no effect.

It coursed into her, feeding the trickle until it flowed
steady. Strong.

A nurse read the data from one of the machines out loud.
The doctor nodded, touched my shoulder. "That's enough.
Let's get her into surgery."

I extinguished the connection, stepped back as they
wheeled the girl out of the room. I closed my eyes, focused on
steadying my breathing. Depending on how much I used,
giving away my energy left me depleted. My breathing was
heavier, my pulse rapid. I felt winded and tired, as if I'd
climbed five flights of stairs.

The two men hugged me, faces teary. "Thank you so
much."

Their gratitude suffused me with warmth. It reminded me
why I'd chosen to become a Powerhouse. "Go be with her."

After they left, the doctor approached me with a hopeful
look. "We have a few more who could use your help if you've
got some time."

I straightened. "Lead the way."

8 STRONGHOLD

After my afternoon classes, I made the drive south into the city's downtown district. Pedestrians crowded the wide walkways leading to and from the skyrail stations. Palm trees speared up alongside streets and in front of buildings.

Mayport had once been a small community within Jacksonville. Since the establishment of the institute, Mayport had flourished into a major city and a homeport for PNs on the east coast.

I opened the diner's door, stepped into a wall of noise. Dinner rush was in full swing, with hungry students and locals piling into the booths. Servers carried trays loaded with mounds of onion rings and burgers piled with toppings. Alternative rock pumped through the speakers in the main dining, while closer to the bar screens broadcasted a local football game.

It'd been ten years since the Battle of St. John's River. Though the city had made a strong comeback, many parts were still cordoned off for repairs. Local business, like Bruce's Burger

Bar, stayed open despite the endless construction and lack of street parking.

Bruce's was a mainstay with the Powerhouse crowd. The locally brewed on tap drinks attracted crowds as much as the oversized burgers and onion rings did. Bartenders worked the taps and leaned against the counter to chat with customers. The air smelled of grilled beef and hot oil.

I found Hector at the far end of the bar, grinning as he leaned in to talk to one of the bartenders, a woman with dusky brown skin. She gave him a coy smile, leaning over the counter.

Hector greeted me as I took the stool beside his. "I was telling Cici about the game next weekend."

"You play?" Cici asked me.

"No."

"Anything from the taps?"

"Club soda."

As she moved off, a small holoscreen flared open in front of me. I scanned my options as Hector and I spent a few minutes catching up.

Our orders arrived a few moments later. The smell of grilled meat made my stomach growl. I stuck to a rigid diet most days. Part of my regime. But I'm not a monster.

I picked up the mammoth burger, took a bite. Savored the exquisite combination of juicy meat, bun, and everything crammed between.

Hector plowed his way through a double order, including behemoth onion rings. PNs have big appetites. Our abilities require a lot of fuel, and eating helped keep the well full.

The energy needs for some, like speedsters and teleporters, were off the charts. When he wasn't working, Hector was either eating or sleeping. Though he always seemed to have enough energy left over to chat up women.

"You got here right on time," he said.

"For what?"

"My new favorite bartender said there's a block party going on downtown tonight. She and her friend need dates."

"Why the hell everyone trying to get me a date?"

"Your sister again?"

"Yeah."

"Didn't the one before the last ask you to get tattoos with her?"

"Don't remind me." Maybe my sister thought I'd be more comfortable with someone who was into what I was, what I did for a living.

The truth was I hated talking about myself as much as I hated hearing someone who didn't know me talk about how much she "liked" me.

"I can't tell Cassi no," I admitted.

Hector polished off his food, ordered dessert. "Since I'm such a good friend, I'm going to give you some advice."

"Listening."

"Arm candy."

"Done listening."

"Someone," he continued. "Who'll go with you to your sister's, pretend to be your girlfriend without any strings."

"A fake girlfriend."

"Exactly. You play it straight, make it a fair deal. Does she need her couch moved or a lawn mowed? A dog to walk?"

"So, business."

"Exactly. I knew a girl who had this guy hounding her. I played boyfriend for a few days. She got him off her case." He used a spoon to point at himself. "I got homemade cupcakes. Pretty good deal."

"It's ludicrous."

"Better than another date with a fangirl in disguise."

He had a point. Still, I couldn't wrap my head around the idea.

A server passed while we were talking. Out of the corner of my eye, I noticed him stop.

I tensed as he started to wobble. Plates full of sizzling food and utensils crowded the tray. The table in front of him was crammed with kids and moms.

The tray careened out of his grasp.

I shoved off the stool, threw myself between it and the kids. My hands braced on either side of the booth, my arms spread wide to catch as many of the missiles as I could. Plates crashed against my back. Forks and knives bounced off.

The people in front of me screamed, the kids wide-eyed. "Alright?" I asked.

One mom gave a jerky nod, clutching her child to her chest. One of the kids bawled.

I joined Hector at the fallen man's side. "Pulse is skippy," he said.

"Oh my God, Wilson!" A woman with a manager's name tag ran over.

"Call 911," I told her, keeping my voice calm and measured. "Then ask everyone to stay back."

Her hands shook as she reached for her HC.

"Guide the paramedics," I said to Hector.

"On it." He vanished in a burst of light and pop of sound.

The bartender, Cici, rushed over to me. "What can I do?"

"Keep a path clear for the paramedics. From here to the door. Get the others to keep everyone seated and calm."

She nodded before taking off. I stayed by the guy's side, administered CPR, keeping my pace steady.

Hector flashed into existence beside me. "They're here."

Paramedics rushed in. They loaded the guy into the ambulance. One of the EMTs kept up a steady stream of conversation. "Hang in there, Wilson. Stay with me."

Memories crashed into me. The taste of blood, the pound of merciless fists into my stomach, my face. My throat raw from screaming. Cassi's terrified expression.

"Nice work." Hector's voice interrupted my thoughts. "You moved quick."

Not fast enough, I thought, watching the ambulance pull away.

People drifted off, speaking in hushed voices. The manager and some customers knelt near the mess, cleaning the spills.

Someone touched my hand. I turned to find a mom from the booth, one of the kids at her side. "Thank you. You protected us."

"You spilled," said the kid, pointing at me.

I reached around my back, felt the sticky slick of ketchup. Chocolate milkshake streamed down my arms.

The woman offered me a wad of napkins. "It's not much."

The kind gesture eased some of the tension out of me. "Not the first shirt I ruined today."

The manager approached me. "Thank you for your help. You boys are welcome back anytime."

"I'll stay," said Hector. "Make sure everyone gets home okay."

We knocked fists. "Good job today," I said.

"All in a day's work."

I found my bag, changed my shirt. Again. Maybe I needed to start carrying more.

I stood on the curb some distance away from the diner, used my HC to call my car. While I waited, I checked my messages.

. . .

PARKCASSILTD: Gave your new date (!) your contact info. Be nice to her! She's beyond sweet.

EVA4EVA: Hi!!!!!!! I'm Eva!

EVA4EVA: Your sister is sweet. You're graduating Powerhouse soon? Beyond! Here's my photo. What do you think? I saw yours, too. HOT. Especially for a SOOFS.

Fuck's sake.

I rubbed the back of my neck. Hector's plan was starting to sound better. But who the hell could I get to agree to such a ridiculous scheme?

I cleared the messages, the previous one rolling up to take its place.

LULLABY: Still on for coffee?

I paused. Debated.

No way. I was letting Hector's bullshit get its hooks in me.

Another ping.

EVA4EVA: Will you be on my Impulse? We can do a couples Q&A!!

EVA4EVA: Pls tell me all about Powerhouse when we meet. I've always wanted to go. I'm a normie, so I just bought the sweatshirt, LOL Can't wait for our date!! *smooches*

.   .   .

I grimaced, sighed. Raked a hand through my hair.
    Finally, I sent a message to Briar.

STRONGHOLD: Busy tonight?

9 LULLABY

B y the end of the week, I was exhausted. I wanted nothing
more than to crawl into bed and sleep for days.

But it was TV night, and TV night is sacred.

Students crowded into the skyrail cab, everyone heading
home or off campus for the weekend. I stayed standing, hooking
an arm around a stanchion. I opened my notes, managed two
seconds of studying before giving up. My brain felt like a
mushy sponge.

Instead, I sent a message to my roommates.

LULLABY: TGIPN
    PURLOIN: + mini CCs!
    INCOGNITO: WGG

It was evening by the time I got back to my building. I took a
moment to appreciate it from the outside. Housing was hard to

come by, especially near the institute. Most of the available places were tiny dorms, overpriced student apartments, or the expensive townhouses closer to the beach.

That's where my friend Hazel came in. She and I met at orientation, where we bonded over the fault "get to know you" games.

"My friend's got a place," she'd said to me. "We're looking for a third."

"Where do you guys live?" I prayed it wasn't out of my price range. "Southcrest?"

"What until you see it."

Benett Tower rose above the surrounding buildings. The elegant silver spire glittered in the evening light, illuminated by countless glass windows. On the front lawn, a holographic logo spun above a low pool, reflecting off the water's surface.

The front doors parted for me, revealing a vast lobby boasting gleaming marble tiles and rich wood furniture. Shining crystals dripped from long chandeliers, giving off a cascading gold light. They hung from high vaulted ceilings alongside enormous mirrors and tall lighted columns. Enormous plants with wide leaves speared out of white vases.

Still hard to believe I'd gone from living in a shoebox sized apartment to a first class condo. I knew Lucie's family owned the building. I was also pretty sure she wasn't charging me and Hazel nearly enough for living there.

A screen activated above the front desk with visitor information. I tapped my HC against the pad on the counter. The electronic voice welcomed me back by name and activated the elevator.

In the elevator, I replayed my meeting with Jase. Would his answer have been different if I hadn't abandoned him? If I'd said something different?

I shook my head. Dwelling on it wouldn't get me anywhere.

I needed to regroup, contact Dr. Singh, figure out my other options.

If there were any.

Music washed over me the moment I stepped inside the apartment. AlterEgo, of course. The foyer opened into a living room with low backed, dove grey seating. Past the floor to ceiling windows, the city sprawled, millions of glittering lights against the dark of night.

The space branched off into two wings on either side, each with its own bathroom. My shoes clicked against gleaming wall to wall wood flooring. Recessed lights cast a creamy glow over the pale gold walls.

I followed the sound of voices into the kitchen. My two roommates stood on either side of the extended counter, singing at the top of their lungs. Behind them, spotless silver appliances gleamed against the dark marble countertops.

Lucie held a bottle of wine, singing as she popped the cork. Her long, straight hair hung in a simple ponytail, deep black against her pale skin. Her mixed Asian and French-American features lit up when she saw me. "Hey! Welcome home."

"I'm mished," Hazel said, setting out glasses. Everything about her made me think of pixies, from her short auburn hair to her petite features. She wore one of her handmade necklaces, the stones a deep forest green against her light skin.

I'd been nervous at first about living with two roommates, but the three of us had become a tight group of friends.

Lucie slapped at my hand when I reached for the cupcakes. "Wait. They need to be perfect."

They seemed fine to me, but Lucie insisted we plate our food like civilized humans. To speed the process, I propped open the pizza boxes. Inhaled the scent of melted cheese, baked crusts, and pepperoni.

We dished up slices and cupcakes then grabbed the wine before heading to the living room.

"Music off," Lucie said as we piled onto the couch. "Screen on, low volume, queue open."

The music died and the wallscreen flared to life, autoplaying our recent show obsession: "Hero Wives," a reality show about normie women who'd married celebrity PNs. Fault, but we were addicted.

"God, that's good," Hazel said, biting into a slice studded with black olives. "The semester's barely started and I'm deaf."

"Me, too." I kicked back, savored the wine while I watched two of the show's leading ladies scream at one another.

"Lucie's not." Hazel fluttered her eyelashes at our roommate. "She's too busy lusting over Dr. Linden."

Lucie blushed. "He's so cute. The glasses, those tweed elbow patches."

I laughed. "Tweed, huh?"

"Ask him out. Seriously," Hazel added when Lucie made a face. "You've been drooling over the guy for over a year now."

"No way he'd say yes. I don't want to make things awkward with my sociology professor."

"Go brave or go home," I said, rubbing her leg. "Or in this case, go tweed or go home."

After two glasses of wine, I spilled about what happened at Dr. Singh's and the dire state of my candidacy.

"What are you going to do now?" Lucie asked. She ate her mini cupcake with a mini fork and somehow didn't look ridiculous.

"Figure out what to do next, I guess."

Hazel gestured with her wine glass. "He didn't even think about it? Fault."

I drank some more wine, not sure of what to say. I was

grateful they took my side, however I couldn't blame Jase for being hesitant.

Thankfully, the new episode ended with some major drama, our other favorite show autoplaying. "Ms. Magnificent," a thriller-action-drama series about a team of women secret agents, some PN and some not.

I leaned forward, riveted. I'd gotten deeply invested in the taut sexual tension between two of the agents.

After, the three of us cleaned, dumping the takeout boxes into the recomposter. It beeped and whirred as it disintegrated everything to base matter and shot them off to be made into new takeout containers or roads or whatever.

I told the others good night and jumped in the shower, using enough vanilla-scented body wash to make the entire bathroom fill with the fragrance. Climbing into my softest pajamas, I made a cup of tea and retreated to my personal sanctuary.

"Setting one," I said as I entered.

The screen activated, playing the soothing, low sound of rain accompanied by a dimmed image of rain falling on leaves. Piles of cream colored pillows covered the soft oatmeal-colored bedspread. Tiny white globe lights hovered in the air, giving everything a dreamy appearance. A diffuser kicked out the gentle scent of cinnamon and vanilla.

I set my tea nearby, climbed into bed, and buried myself in the pillows. Wallowed in softness and comfort. Rolling onto my back, I opened a screen, scrolled for an ebook to read.

A message pinged. I sat up, eyes widening.

STRONGHOLD: Busy tonight?

·   ·   ·

I stared, mind spinning. Was he calling to turn me down?
I hurried to message him back.

LULLABY: What's up?
STRONGHOLD: I need to talk to you.

10 STRONGHOLD

I found a bench in the small park next to Briar's building, a tall, shining tower spearing up into the night sky. Palm trees lining the streets rustled in a breeze that carried the scent of the ocean.

While I waited, I studied my notes for an upcoming exam. Tough to concentrate, considering. I'd spent the entire ride over thinking about what to say.

Whatever Hector might think, there is no right way to say, "I want you to be my fake girlfriend."

I should've gone home, suffered through whatever torment this date would bring me. But two more texts from EVA4EVA had driven me to the point of desperation.

Besides, I was starting to realize if I didn't at least make some attempt, my sister was going to stick with this dating scheme until I lost my sanity.

Briar emerged from the building not long after I arrived. Her blonde hair hung in a loose braid. In a pale blue hoodie and matching pajama pants, she looked comfortable.

And soft. And pretty.

I studied the design on her pants. "Sloths?"

"Pajamas are required for TGIPN. That's 'Thank God It's Premiere Night.'"

"Sloth ones?"

She grinned. "Sorry I can't invite you in. Strict, 'no boys on TV nights allowed' policy."

We sat on the bench, a few inches between us. This close, I caught the scent of vanilla lingering on her skin. "A tough organization."

"And exclusive." She took in a deep breath. "I love this place at night."

"You're from out of state?"

"Not far. Near Savannah." She nudged me with her elbow. A friendly gesture. "What about you?"

"My parents travel a lot."

"Career PNs?"

"Both of them."

"That's impressive. You must be proud."

"I--" My jaw tightened. I wasn't here to talk about my parents. I'd gotten too relaxed. Sitting with Briar in the warm air. The night quiet around us. I'd dropped my guard.

I pulled it back into place. "I wanted to talk to you."

She tensed. "You said it's about the project."

"Yes. And, ah, something else." I drummed my fingers against my knee. "I need a date."

Her brows lifted. "Need?"

I stood, paced a few steps. "I need to get into this night club and it's a Couple's Only event."

"Whoa." Briar leaned back, her eyes widening.

"Damn it." I raked a hand through my hair. "I'm not explaining this right."

Briar stepped in front of me, making me stop. She touched

my arm, the barest brush of skin. "Why don't you start at the beginning?"

I sat, waited for her to settle beside me before giving a brief, and very annotated, version of my problem.

She toyed with the end of her braid, her expression thoughtful. "In summary," she said. "You need a temporary girlfriend so your sister will get off your case."

"That's the gist."

"You need a date." She met my gaze. Held. "Turns out I need a partner for a project."

Relief flooded me. "That I can do."

"Why me? You must have friends who are girls."

I didn't. In my experience, the less complicated my life, the better.

Out loud, I said, "Figured you'd agree if I promised to partner with you."

"Then you figured right." She straightened her legs and I caught a flash of her socks above her shoes. More sloths. "When do we go?"

"That easy?"

"Why not? You need help, and I need a partner. Simple. And besides, it might be kind of fun."

I shifted on the bench. "Briar, I want to be honest with you."

The wind gusted, slapping right into our faces. Lose dust and bits of grass kicked through the air hard enough to sting.

I put an arm around her, tugged her close. Briar squeezed her eyes shut, pressing against my side. When the wind stopped, she opened her eyes, stared up at me.

"Being honest is good," she whispered. A faint flushed worked its way over her cheeks.

Her vanilla scent gripped me by the throat. It made me want to lean in close. Take a deep breath. A big bite.

"I can't get involved with anyone," I said, trying to get the image of taking a taste of Briar out of my head. The wind pulled some of her hair from the tie. My hands burned with the desire to work the rest of those golden strands loose.

Dammit, why'd she have to smell so good? Feel so good?

My voice came out rough. "No strings attached."

"Sure." She sounded a little breathless. "It's a busy time right now. Work and candidacy. Saving lives."

"Exactly."

She swallowed, the motion drawing my attention to the smooth lines of her neck. The two of us had at some point leaned toward one another. My arm was still around her, holding her to me. The neckline of her pajamas slipped, offering me a hint of smooth skin and enticing cleavage.

Clearing my throat, I drew my arm away. "As long as we both get it."

"Yeah, I get it." She eased back from me. The wind rushed between us, cooling the place where her warmth had seeped into me.

"Send me the link to the club. And to your previous dates," Briar said as we rose.

"Why?"

"Your sister picked them, right? She must think they're your type."

She had a point. The more realistic we were, the more likely my sister would buy it.

"I'm warning you," I said, using my HC to send her the links. "Some of them are intense."

"Of course. A guy like you probably draws a lot of intense love interests."

"Guy like me?"

"Never mind. Here's hoping I make a good fake girlfriend."

"I bet you're a great girlfriend."

"My exes might not agree. Maybe this will be good practice. Speaking of which." She glanced down to my hands, back up to my face. "Are we going to be, you know, affectionate?"

"We don't have to do anything you don't want to."

"Won't it look weird?"

"We'll tell my sis you've got a hands off policy."

"Like a piece of museum art?"

"Or food at the counter. Display purposes only." She laughed, and the light sound thrilled me. More of her braid unraveled, leaving the tie dangling from the ends.

I grabbed it without thinking, gently tugging it free. The loosened strands fell against her shoulder, enticing me to touch.

Briar leaned closer, her chin tipping up. "We should probably get used to close proximity. For appearances' sake."

My jaw tensed. "Tell me if I cross a line. Deal?"

"So many deals tonight."

"Briar."

"I'll tell you." She slid closer, leaving no space between us. Her breasts pressed against my chest, her palms sliding up to rest on my shoulders.

She lifted onto her toes, close enough her breath tickled against my skin. Her lashes lowered, fanning over her cheekbones. Pale brown freckles scattered across her nose like gold dust.

Unable to resist, I cupped her face in my palms, lowered my mouth to hers.

She made a soft sound against my mouth, as if eating something delicious. The taste of her had my blood roaring for more. I imagined sitting back on the bench. Parting her legs and making her straddle my lap. Biting her neck while my hands explored her body.

She stepped back. "Not bad. Right?"

I ignored the hammering of my heart. "Nothing I can't handle."

"Same. Same for me."

I walked her to the front of the building. She paused as the doors parted for her. "See you tomorrow."

"See you." I stayed in place, watching until she was out of sight.

As I drove home, I used my car's dash to send my sister a message.

STRONGHOLD: I've got a date for the thing.
PARKCASSILTD: ???
STRONGHOLD: Sorry for the last minute notice. I'll apologize to Eva.
PARKCASSILTD: Again, ???

I chuckled. After a moment, I added:

STRONGHOLD: Can't wait for you to meet her.

More messages from my sister rolled in. I let them pile up, staring out the window. In one day, I'd landed myself in a partner project I didn't have time for and gotten a girlfriend I didn't know how to deal with.

Fake girlfriend, I reminded myself. A lover was out of the deal for me. No attachments. No promises.

I steeled my determination, resolving to keep things strictly business.

No matter how much Briar tempted to take more.

11 LULLABY

BRIANWILLIAMS: How's networking going? It's important to make connections early on.

Did "fake girlfriend" count as a connection?

I pondered the question all during my Sociology of Family Dynamics class. We took a lot of typical classes at the institute. Psych 101, communications, english. We also took stuff like Advanced Laser Techniques in Close Combat Training and Intergalactic Conflict Management.

Normally I enjoyed attending lectures. But it was the day of my first date with Jase. Between my nerves and mini freak outs, I got one out of ten words the professor said, making my notes for the day sparse. Hopefully I could fill in the gaps before midterms.

After the lecture, the rest of the class filed out, shouldering bags, opening screens, speaking in low voices. I took the stairs to the podium. "Dr. Linden, my paper."

"Yes, I got it last night. Good work."

"Thanks for letting me submit it a day late. The hospital asked me to work extra shifts last week."

"Everyone gets one pass on late assignments. Sudden emergencies certainly aren't uncommon around here. And you wrote with obvious enthusiasm for the topic."

Enthusiasm wasn't the word I'd use. Dr. Linden's classes focused on the history and social dynamics between PNs, latents, and normies. I'd written about the relationship between my uncle, my father, and myself. I guess I'd let my emotions come through my words.

"I don't mean to overreach, but if you need help, there are resources on campus to help those with difficult situations at home."

"I can handle it."

He sighed. "There it is, the Powerhouse 'push through' attitude. I'm latent, however I've seen too many young heroes take on too much at once. Success in the present at the cost of longterm sustainability isn't success at all."

"You say some good stuff sometimes."

"Part of the job description. Pedantic as they are, I hope you'll take my words to heart."

"I will, professor."

"Good." He cleared his throat, turned red. "Perhaps I might ask you for some advice. Your friend, Lucie."

"Oh?" I grinned when he blushed.

"She asked me out for a meal, which is like a date, right?"

"Exactly like that."

He scratched his chin. "It's been so long for me. Not since my fiancée died."

"She was an amazing hero." Though I'd been a child at the time, I'd mourned with the rest of the city when the news of Steelstar's death went public.

His eyes crinkled. "She was. My primary concern is Lucie won't enjoy herself with me."

"It's cliche and unhelpful, but be yourself."

"I'm just a sociology professor."

"That's what Lucie wants. Although you could wear something cool and casual to change things up."

"Oh, God, clothes." When I laughed, he smiled. "Thank you, Briar. My door's open if you want to talk."

"Thanks, Dr. Linden."

I left him muttering to himself about the benefits of jeans over trousers. Stopping at the on-campus grill and snack bar, I grabbed a sandwich, devoured it on the way back to the condo.

No time to waste when getting combat ready.

An hour later, the three of us crammed into the condo's main bathroom. I say "crammed" but the bathroom alone was the size of my freshman year dorm room. The huge stretch of mirror reflected the gleaming marble tiles and hanging orb lights.

Even the bathrooms had wallscreens. The one beside the mirror was currently playing music, the screen displaying little water droplets bursting in time with the beat. The bottom read out gave the time and weather conditions.

The fresh scent of citrus cleaner clung to the sparkling countertops. A box of mint chocolate cookies and a plate of sliced apples balanced near the faucet next to cans of Rocket Water, cran-rasp-lime flavor.

I sat on the edge of the tub, wearing nothing except a strapless bra and panties. My bare feet, toes painted bright pink, dug into the soft green mats. Half of my hair was clipped, the other half hanging in limp, wet strands. Hazel spritzed me with my favorite perfume. It clung to my damp skin, making the room smell of musky vanilla.

I eyed the whirling, buzzing rod in Lucie's hand. "That's going in my hair, right?"

"Of course!" She pressed a button. The device buzzed louder.

"Are you sure it's safe?"

"Would I hurt you?"

"Physically or emotionally?"

Hazel grumbled as she sifted through an enormous make up bag. "Where the hell is the lip dye?" She grabbed the bag, upended the contents into the sink. Little bottles, colorful containers, and brushes of every size clattered against the porcelain. Something powdery exploded, streaking the sink with dusty pink splotches.

Hazel poked through the pile, sending makeup items clattering up and down the sides of the sink. "Ah ha!" She lifted a tube in triumph. "Found it."

"Yay," I said.

As Lucie started on my hair, I noticed the bright gleam in her eyes. "Someone's chipper. Tweed elbow patches have anything to do with it?"

Hazel gasped. "You asked him. Finally."

"I did."

The three of us whooped and clapped. Lucie waved the curler dangerously close to my head as she did a little dance. "We're going to dinner. I want to keep it casual, no pressure."

"He's excited," I said.

"Not as excited as I am."

I hoped their date went well. Lucie had been interested in the professor for over a year already, and Linden needed some joy in his life. A lot of superheroes had been lost in the Battle of St. John's. The most elite groups were still rebuilding their numbers.

I shifted, jiggled my leg. Part of me wanted to stay home,

curl up, and binge watch movies. I was already regretting my decision to go to this club. I'm the girl who shows up to class in sweats, her hair wet from the shower. I don't mind the occasional glam night, but something about the fuss was making me nervous.

Maybe it was the idea of going on a date with Jase. Something passed between us the night we'd made the deal. I'd gone away thinking about his arm around me, the quiet intensity in his eyes.

Would he be that way in bed? Forceful focus and silent passion? The mental image of him over me, inside me, made my thighs clench.

Fake date, I reminded myself. We'd made it clear this was for the sake of fooling his sister. And, in exchange, I was getting my project partner. We'd both get what we wanted, no strings attached. End of story.

Then why the strange sense of disappointment?

Why did I keep imagining us as more?

12 LULLABY

Lucie grabbed a lock of my hair and began twisting it with the scary buzzy wand thing. "Trust me, you're going to look beyond."

I tried to ignore the alarming amount of steam rising from my hair. Luckily, I had the distraction of Hazel mashing a beauty sponge against my cheeks to distract me. She ordered from one pose to another. Tilt my chin, suck in my cheeks. Look up, look down.

Hazel studied my features, then glanced at Lucie. "Ultimate?"

"Definitely." The tool in Lucie's hand buzzed. More steam billowed.

"Wait, what does that mean?" I startled as another tinier, spikier brush loomed toward my eye.

"Relax," said Hazel. "We're experts."

"Expert torturers," I muttered, admiring my hands. The cuticles were smooth and they'd added slender stripes of deep pink on top of nude polish. Pretty.

My mind drifted while I let them work their sorcery on me.

Maybe I was nervous because I hadn't been on a date in forever. And I'd be faking it in front of his family.

My throat tightened. Even the thought of trying to be someone's arm candy made me queasy. In my first year, I'd forced myself to attend parties with my boyfriend. He believed staying home was boring. I didn't want to be the wet blanket, the one who brought everyone down. Instead, I played the party girl.

I'd hated it. The forced cheerfulness, the endless hours of socializing with people I didn't care about. I'd been relieved when we broke up.

It was another reason my career was important to me. Yes, it was demanding and competitive. The hours were brutal and the assignments impossible. Not every candidate made it. Many dropped out due to burnout or failing to meet requirements.

But I was finally doing something I wanted to do. Something for myself. Plus, if I hadn't come to the institute, I'd have never met Lucie and Hazel. I'd explained everything to them and they'd offered to help me get ready.

Except I hadn't told them about the kiss.

My cheeks burned remembering it. God, what had I been thinking? Relationship practice, desensitization, possession by ghosts. No matter how I spun it, there'd been no reason for me to kiss him. For me to want to kiss him.

Except he'd been so close. His eyes intense as he stared at me. His soft lips, his chest firm and unyielding against my breasts. He'd looked half angry, half confused, half aroused, which was too many halves but somehow added up to one sexy, brooding expression.

Hazel frowned. "You're kind of flushed. Feeling okay?"

"Fine," I squeaked. "Hot from the curler thingy." I'm not a good liar. A fact I perhaps should've told Jase.

My HC pinged. I scowled at the message. "One second."

"Hurry, your hair will dry weird."

"Heaven forbid." Leaving the bathroom, I went to the end of the hallway. Making sure only my head showed, I accepted the call.

"Briar." Uncle Brian frowned. "What in the world?"

"Girl stuff. Hair stuff."

"You have time for such foolishness?"

I swallowed a howl of rage. "What's up?"

"Your father and I have been thinking."

Which meant Uncle Brian had been thinking and somehow got my dad to go along with it. I held my tongue, though. The less I interrupted him, the faster the call would end.

"You should apply for the summer semester program. Take extra classes."

"We talked about this." I fought for patience. "I want to work."

"You won't get another chance like this. If I had half the opportunities you have, I'd—"

"Got to go, my hair's going to dry weird."

He narrowed his eyes. "Fine, but we're not done talking about this."

I ended the call, took a moment to lean against the wall with my eyes shut.

When the frustration had passed, I returned to the bathroom. Hazel was telling a story and eating a snack at the same time.

Lucie laughed, then turned to me as I entered. "Everything okay?"

"Yep." I plopped back on the tub's edge, glad for the night out. At least it would keep my mind off things. "Do your thing."

Lucie hummed as she clipped and curled her way around

my head. Hazel poked at my bottom lip with her ring finger, stepped back, stepped in to poke some more.

"Done," she said at last. "All that's left is the dress."

I glanced at the dress hanging from the towel hook. A short, rich blue number I'd ordered online. When it shifted, it gave off iridescent flashes of vivid pink. The shoes were a shimmering rich pink with needle thin heels.

With their help, I climbed into the dress, adjusted my strapless bra, slipped on the shoes. My roommates nodded as if admiring a piece of art.

"Faultless," said Hazel.

I turned the mirror. "Whoa, my lashes."

"Like a baby giraffe." Lucie grinned. "Or a dik-dik!"

"Ugh-ugh," I said. Although the lashes were stellar. And my hair did this tumbly-curly-glossy thing.

"Photo time," Hazel said.

We spent the next few minutes singing songs and taking photos. Making stupid faces, piling into the tub. We took more shots of the counter we'd destroyed with makeup products and snacks. For a time, I forgot about the deal I'd made, my classes, assignments, my situation at home.

The screen chimed, a notification flashing that someone requested our floor.

The girls looked at one another. Then they shoved me out of the bathroom.

"Go on!" Hazel hissed. "We'll clean up in here."

Stifling a groan, I waited in the foyer, tried not to fidget.

The elevator opened. Jase stood on the other side. He wore dark trousers and an open, tailored jacket in deep charcoal grey over a black shirt. He'd rolled the sleeves, exposing the lean muscles in his forearms.

He'd shaved, leaving the hard line of his jaw clean. I caught the faint whiff of soap and shaving cream. Woodsy and masculine.

I stopped myself from licking my lips. "Hi," I said.

He frowned, his brows drawing together. "Ready?" The word came out clipped.

My smile faltered. "Let me grab my purse."

I spun away from the door, taking the time to compose myself. What was I expecting? For him to gush over me or say I looked hot? Okay, would've been nice. I'd figured on inviting him in, offering a beverage. Try to get to know him a little better.

His tone and cool reaction made it clear. I had to remember this was a transaction. Jase wasn't interested in me. For him, this was strictly business.

I grabbed my bag, took a deep breath, and steeled myself for the night ahead.

13 LULLABY

We rode the elevator in silence. Jase stood ramrod straight, his eyes fixed straight ahead. His expression guarded, his brows drawn together. The guy looked like he was heading to an execution rather than a night out.

His car, Ace, activated as we drew near, the doors sliding open.

Jase took my hand, surprising me. "Watch your step." His touch was gentle, his hand large and warm.

"Thanks," I said, easing into the car. The door slid closed and I watched Jase circle around the front to the side.

I bit my lip. One second, he was cold and standoffish. The next, he was all attentive gentleman. A confusing mix.

He slid behind the console and the car chirped. Jase gave it the go ahead and the vehicle slid onto the street. Music queued, something chill and electronic.

"You do listen to music," I said.

"Thought you might like it."

It beat silence. And it was nice, listening to it together. I was surprised he wasn't making me use the fancy audio/controller ear pieces so he could stew in brooding silence.

I fought to settle down and not tug at my skirt. Every time I squirmed, it inched further up my thighs.

"Cold?"

"I'm fine." A laugh escaped me. "God, this is worse than prom."

His expression softened. Not quite a smile, but close. "Tell me about it."

"Did yours have a theme?"

"Casino night."

"As bad as it sounds?"

"Didn't go." Before I asked why, he added, "What about yours?"

"Fairy tale. They even brought a live horse with a horn tied to its forehead."

"Seriously?"

"Oh, yeah. Couples could sit on it, take photos. Sounds romantic until the horse starts shitting everywhere. The prom queen stepped right in it."

His mouth curved. "No way."

"Three inch stilettos versus a huge pile of poop. She threw a fit and had to be escorted out."

"Sounds memorable."

"It was for her."

We lapsed into silence for a few minutes, the music pumping through the speakers. The highway sped past, illuminated by the headlights of other cars.

Hard to believe I'd been in the same seat a week prior, struggling to change into my bodysuit. Now I was wearing a party dress and zooming off to a night club.

Not just any night club. The opening of Iceberg had been much anticipated by the city's nightlife crowd. The club's

Impulse page was full of hype about the owner, celebrity entrepreneur Cassi Park.

My stomach jittered. I hadn't realized when I'd signed up to be a fake girlfriend how beyond his sister was. Then again, her brother was Jase. Must've run in the family. I'd have to work hard to dazzle her.

Even more impressive were the women she'd attempted to match with him. A Pilates instructor, a candidate for the Olympic ski team, the founder of a successful line of beauty products.

I didn't begrudge them their accomplishments, and I didn't want to change who I was. Still, it was intimidating knowing I was going to be compared to them.

A memory crashed into me. My boyfriend's by then familiar eye roll whenever I'd hesitated to attend yet another party.

My chest squeezed. I gripped my clutch and stared at the highway outside. Gage's behavior had left me miserable and full of shame. Days passed before I understood what a huge bag of dicks he was.

"We should talk about the project," Jase said, breaking the silence.

"Right." I flicked open the screen of my HC, poked around until I found the file. "It says we need a focal topic, plus the supervision of a faculty member."

At least we had that part covered. Dr. Singh was pumped to hear we were working together. She was banking on us being a success.

No pressure or anything.

"What's your area of focus?" I asked.

"Crisis and disaster."

The most dangerous stuff, second only to being an Aegis agent. Crisis work was for hard core PNs, the ones who lived the whole "hero" mentality. The rate of burnout was sky high.

"Yours?" he asked.

"Specialized assistance. Career wise, I want to be a life coach."

"It suits you. You're easy to talk to."

The praise caught me off guard. I'd thought he was closed off, but maybe for him, this was a lot of talking.

"Dr. Singh added some suggestions." I flicked through the list, read them out loud. We debated some of the options, came up with some of our own. In addition to the periodic write ups and reports, we each had to submit a separate recap of our experiences.

Our areas of focus were vastly different. We had to find a common middle ground. I guess that was the point of the program, to explore and get to know branches different from your own.

"What about counseling following a crisis?" I said. "Finding resources after a disaster for PNs who've worked in crisis situations. We need help, too, sometimes."

Jase's hand fisted. "Yeah," he said, his voice rough.

I tensed. "Did I step in some horse poop?"

"It's nothing." The words came out hard, clipped. Definitely shutting down any possibility of discussion.

But Jase and I were going to be working together for months. It'd be nice to learn something about him other than he ate healthy and owned a nice car.

Did he like to read? How did he feel about pineapple on pizza? Favorite flavor of Rocket Water?

The two of us sat in silence, my screen casting a pale blue glow in front of me.

Rather than make things worse, I activated my HC's

keyboard, typed a few notes on what we'd discussed. "I'll shoot you a copy of what we went over."

"Appreciate it." After a moment, he added, "It's a good idea."

Some of the tension in my shoulders eased. "Okay, we'll start there."

We discussed a few more possibilities, though the awkwardness lingered in the air. The car cruised underneath the arching sign marking the beginning of the city's downtown district. Red brick buildings lined the streets, housing everything from restaurants to pubs, lounges to nightclubs. Street lamps, crowned with fat white bulbs cast a dreamy glow over the sidewalks.

Tourists clustered outside restaurants, studying the prices offered by holo-menus. College students emerged from one bar to duck into another not ten feet away. A group of women wearing pink t-shirts reading "Bridesmaid" whooped as they pushed a woman in a white t-shirt along in a hovercart.

The car eased up to an empty space along the curb. Jase got out, reached my door as it slid open. He cupped my elbow in his palm, steadying me as I climbed out.

A thrill danced over my skin. The spark I'd felt the night we'd kissed caught hold, became a low flame that warmed my blood.

I attempted a smile, hoping my voice sounded light. "You're a great fake boyfriend."

"That's praise?"

"Gotta work your way up."

"I'll do my best." He paused before extending his hand to me.

Charmed, I laced our fingers together. He signaled the car and it slid off, joining the streaming rows of traffic.

Music pumped from one of the establishments, something

low and throbbing. A food truck on the corner stood with windows open. The unmistakable aroma of fish tacos and fried potatoes filled the air.

We joined the flow of the crowd heading for his sister's nightclub. The building next to it housed some kind of fusion restaurant, CNSNNT. The holo-menu flared to life as we passed by.

"What the hell is 'SPRGS?'" Jase asked. He ran the letters together so it came out "spergs."

"I think it's 'asparagus' with the vowels taken out." I scanned the other menu items, which included 'CVCH' and 'GRLLD SLMN WTH LMN BSL VNGRTT.'

Jase's voice and expression stayed flat. "Delicious."

I laughed, gave his arm an appreciative squeeze.

It was like trying to squeeze a rock. His hard muscles didn't give an inch. It made me wonder what he might look like shirtless.

Or, even better, naked.

Past the restaurant loomed "Iceberg." The part brick, part steel building gleamed with low white and turquoise lights. More lights lit the walkway from underneath and a blast of cool air blew from above. I shivered as chilled air flowed over my ankles and across my bare legs.

Jase skirted the line, escorting me to the guys flanking the door. "Park, Jase."

"Welcome, Mr. Park, to Iceberg." The other guy held open the door, gave me a respectful nod. "We hope you and your date have an enjoyable evening."

Seems this fake girlfriend thing had its perks.

14 STRONGHOLD

"A ren't you supposed to slip them money?" Briar asked as we passed the bouncers.

"We're VIPs."

"My favorite letters. Right next to 'spergs.'"

I laughed. Despite myself, I enjoyed Briar's company. When she listened, her eyes focused on mine, her head tilted a little to one side. She'd lean in, as if whatever I was saying fascinated her.

My stomach tightened when I remembered her opening the door. She might as well have punched me in the gut. Soft, tousled curls. Those big, baby blues. That sweet scent.

It drove me crazy every time she squirmed in the car, dragging that short, strapless number higher up her legs. Those creamy, soft thighs begged to be stroked. Licked. Bitten.

Music thumped through the walls as we followed the short corridor past the entranceway. The corridor opened to the main dance floor. Dark wood panels lined the walls of the open space. Rows of lights cast dreamy glows over hand painted murals.

More lights strobed over the main area where a throng of people danced and writhed. Hair and limbs whipped, feet pounded. The music filled the air in a physical wave, pounding into my bones. Smaller levitating dance floors floated, carrying more dancers.

Other patrons squeezed past us in the narrow corridor. Briar shifted, bumping my side.

Untangling our fingers, I pressed my palm to her lower back, slid it around her waist.

"Tell me if I do something not okay," I said.

"So far, so good," she said, her cheeks flushing.

I tucked her against my side and we made our way around the perimeter. Low lounge benches ringed the room, pale white against the dark walls. People sat sipping colorful drinks and leaning in close to share conversation. Servers gathered empty glasses, brought fresh cocktails.

The music changed, pumping thick and fast. The live DJ stood on a hoverplatform floating above the main floor. Her station, a sleek white number, flickered and pulsed in time with the beats.

"This is amazing," Briar said. Her mouth curved in an awed smile.

"Want to dance?"

"You dance?"

"My sister requires it when I visit. It's mostly bobbing up and down. Occasional hands in the air."

Seeing Briar's grin made me glad I'd offered.

We edged onto the dance floor, let ourselves get absorbed by the crowd. The beat shifted to something more euphoric. The lights changed to match, cascading in a rain effect. Cooled air drifted from above in clouds.

Briar swayed and shimmied in front of me, enjoying herself

rather than worrying about form. Sometimes, she'd meet my gaze and make silly exaggerated movements.

I chuckled, indulged myself by running my hands down her back. In response, her arms slid up my chest, around my neck. Our bodies pressed close. Close enough I could see the lights reflecting in her eyes. Goosebumps stood out on her arms from the cool air. I rubbed her skin and she shivered.

"Cold?" I asked.

"No." She bit her lip. "I'm not."

I tensed, fingers gripping her hips. "I'm trying to be a gentleman."

"It's difficult right now?"

"You're fucking right it is."

She leaned against me, curves molding to my body.

Growling, I grabbed her wrist, spun her around. She yelped when I caught her waist, pulled her back against my front.

"You feel way too good against me." I closed my arms around her middle under her breasts.

She rocked back, her ass molding to my front. "Jase."

I tightened my hold, thrilled when she gasped. I wanted to kiss her. Kiss her until she said my name again. Wanted to lift up the back of her skirt, find out what she wore underneath. Let my hands roam upward to the front of her dress. Drag it down to spill her breasts.

Instead, I exhaled, fought to get a handle on myself. We were getting swept up in the music, the atmosphere. That was all.

"Let's get a drink." I grabbed her hand to lead her from the dance floor, taking the time to let my pulse come back to normal.

An expansive bar filled the opposite end of the room. The sides of it were jagged, glowing a soft white, making it look like a glacier. The counter on top of it spanned smooth and sleek, a gleaming black against the white.

As we approached, a holoscreen rose out of the counter, displaying the cocktail menu.

"No 'spergs,' said Briar.

"Afraid not." I rested my hands on the bar on either side of her. I should've stepped back, given us both some space. But I couldn't stop myself from touching her.

She leaned back against me, her eyes fixed on the menu. "Ooh, chocolatini." She tapped the selection.

I chose a club soda with lime. The menu thanked us before fading.

"Straight-laced as ever," said a bartender, approaching us. Natural curls fluffed and fell around a face with medium brown skin and brown eyes. "We don't see enough of you around here."

"Briar, this is Alba Rivers. My sister's girlfriend."

"Nice to meet you."

"Same. We were thrilled Jase brought a date."

"I'm thrilled to be here." Briar gave a strained smile.

I rubbed a hand over her back, hoping to ease some of the tension there. I hadn't considered how uncomfortable this would be for her. How the hell had Hector made it sound easy?

"I'll have your drink ready in a moment." Alba paused, leaned in. "Extra chocolate."

"My two favorite words."

Alba laughed, then said to me, "Your sister was hoping to talk to you one on one for a moment. She's in the office."

I glanced at Briar.

"It's okay. Go ahead."

"You sure?"

Alba slid a drink onto the bar, a the little skewer balanced across its surface. Instead of olives, it held three tiny chocolate truffles.

Briar popped one into her mouth, made an appreciative noise. "Definitely sure."

"I'll keep an eye on her," said Alba. No doubt the second I left, she'd be drilling Briar for details.

Aware of Alba's gaze, I paused to brush my lips against Briar's temple. "Be right back."

She turned red. "Me, too. I mean, I'll be here."

God, she was cute. I wanted to hear what other nonsense she'd spill if I kissed her for real. If I let my hands explore her body the way they wanted to.

I headed for the stairs, grateful for the distance. Whatever this raw chemistry was between me and Briar, I needed to put an end to it.

15 LULLABY

I slid onto a stool and watched Jase climb the stairs to the second floor. The phantom heat from his touch, his body, lingered on my skin. I'd wanted to run my hands over the rest of his muscles to see if they were as rock hard. Exchange a kiss. A real one this time.

At least it wasn't just me. I'd thought he was immune to my charms because of his cold reaction to our kiss and my dress. But according to him, he was working hard to control himself.

Getting a glimpse of what lay behind his guarded demeanor was tantalizing. Like the dimple, an elusive, rare sighting. And when he'd pressed his erection against my ass, my sex had given one long, hard pulse. Knowing I stirred him up made my blood hum.

A bad sign. The two of us had made an agreement to not get involved. Jase was strong enough to shrug off the heat between us. Was I?

"How's the drink?" Alba asked.

I dragged my attention to the present, took a tentative sip. The sweet, luscious taste of chocolate, creamy liquor, and vodka washed over my tongue. The drink was rich, the chocolate decadent. Liquid, boozy dessert.

Alba grinned. "Good, isn't it?"

"Beyond." I popped another tiny truffle into my mouth. Hazelnut filling.

"It's one of my specialities. Cassi has a real sweet tooth."

"Same here. Maybe we'll get along." If I got Alba on my side, hopefully Cassi would be easier.

"Sure you will." Alba set another skewer of minuscule truffles onto a tiny dish, slid the dish over to me. "Here. You're on the house tonight."

"Thanks." Unresolved sex fantasies aside, this VIP girlfriend thing was pretty sweet. "How'd you meet Cassi?"

"At a bartending competition. I was a contender."

"Did you win?"

"Yep." She shrugged it off. As if everyone went around winning bartending competitions. "Cassi was recruiting for her first club. I won her over with my tiramisu cocktail."

"Ooh, sounds good."

While we chatted, her hands kept moving. Flipping bottles, wiping surfaces, stacking glasses. Each movement smooth and fluid, with the easy grace and confidence of a pro who did this for a living.

Alba the champion bartender. Cassi the savvy business owner. Jase, who was good at, well, everything.

Meanwhile, I'd eaten cold, naked spaghetti noodles for breakfast and was two years behind on laundry.

The pressure to impress weighed on me. What if Cassi didn't find me good enough for her brother? If I didn't pull off the fake girlfriend thing, would Jase back out of our deal?

Plus, I wanted to help him. It's my Powerhouse nature.

Alba mixed something purple and lime green, passed it to a waiting server. "How'd you and Jase meet?"

Here we go. "We both go to the institute. Have the same advisor. Met in the elevator on the way to her office, actually."

"Aww, sounds like a romantic movie."

I thought about Jase passed out on the elevator floor. "Exactly like that." I took another swallow of my drink for courage. "We met up for coffee after and things took off."

The words came out smoothly enough. Not quite a lie, either. Isn't that what people say? To mix in some truths?

"Nice to see Jase having fun for once. He could use it."

"That's what I said to him. The other day. I said, 'Let's do something fun for a change.' And he said, 'Yes, let's.' Now, here we are. Fun."

Okay, not so smooth after all.

"What do you guys do together?"

His previous setups flashed through my mind. I considered something impressive, but if I said something like "para-sailing" she might assume I'm an expert and ask me questions. Better to stick with something familiar.

"We've been binge-watching 'Ms. Magnificent.' Getting ready for the new season."

Alba's brows drew together. "Interesting. He's not much for TV."

Damn. I gave a half-hearted laugh. Drank some more of my cocktail.

"You're different from most of his other dates." She said it while smiling, obviously intending it as a compliment.

My stomach dropped. I was bombing this. The game plan had been to present myself as a great fake girlfriend, one who suited him.

But I was bad at lying. At trying to be someone I wasn't. It was too much like my miserable freshman year of trying to please my boyfriend, my dad, my uncle.

Alba moved off to fill more orders. Glad for the respite, I

nursed my drink, glanced over at the stairs. They climbed to a walled loft with dark tinted windows.

I wondered what Jase was saying about me to his sister. No way he was uttering gibberish the way I was. Plus I couldn't shake the impression I was coming across as lackluster. Boring.

I had to get a grip. Whatever the outcome, I'd made Jase a promise. I wasn't going to back out of our deal now.

I leaned against the bar, watching the dancers, chatting with Alba whenever she wasn't filling orders. I finished my drink, contemplated trying something fruity with rum. The chocolate and alcohol swirled in my system, giving me a pleasant buzz.

Right then, an AlterEgo song came on, the DJ spinning it into a thumping remix. I leaned in to tell Alba I how much I loved this song.

"I fucking hate this song."

I spun, wondering who it was and how dare they. My jaw dropped at the sight of the man walking towards the bar, his arm slung around the neck of a gorgeous woman with cherry red hair. My breath caught, the drink I'd consumed churning in my stomach.

Gage was as handsome as ever. Classic heartthrob features, pale skin, brown eyes. Dark hair meticulously groomed to look as if it wasn't. He wore an expensive black suit, the buttons of his white dress shirt undone enough to give him a casual appearance.

He froze when he saw me, features twisting into a snarl. "Briar? What the fuck are you doing here?"

16 STRONGHOLD

The stairs led to a loft extending over the bar area. I climbed the staircase, the metal steps ringing underfoot. The pounding music receded behind me to a dull throb, the flickering lights giving way to a steady glow from the wall lights.

The door read "Authorized Personnel Only." I rapped against it, then pushed it opened when I heard it unlatch.

It opened to a sizable room that could've served as a separate lounge. The opposite wall was one large window overlooking the club. Below, the crowd surged, undulating in a living wave.

Wide chairs ranged around a square table to create a seating area. Glass cubes sat in the center of the table, each one housing a low, flickering flame. A wallscreen spanned the space above a mini bar and kitchenette area, stocked with glasses, liquor, and a single serve coffee maker. A brown paper bag of takeout food sat on the counter.

Instead of ceiling lights, long, thin bulbs hung at regular intervals along the walls. The same music pumping on the dance floor piped through the screen at a low volume, creating a backdrop of sound.

My sister sat at the far end of the room at a sleek black wrap around desk. A candle burned at her elbow, throwing off the fresh scent of eucalyptus.

"You made it!" The screen in front of her closed as she stood. She darted around the desk and put her arms around me. She was almost as tall as me, and wearing heels made up for the difference. Her deep purple top was tucked into trim black pants. Her manager look.

Some of the tension drained out of me. She'd never manifested abilities herself, had nothing except pride for me and my chosen path.

Seeing her reminded me about why I had to keep my head in the game.

"What do you think? Did you get a chance to look around?"

"It's amazing." Pride flooded me. Iceberg was her second club, and if the line outside was any indicator, it was already a success.

She beamed. "Thanks! I've got some takeout here. Stuffed mushrooms, they're beyond. Eat some, they're good for you. I know I didn't always eat the best when I was your age."

Though she was barely five years ahead of me, I let her fuss for a few moments. It didn't matter how old I got or much I assured her I was doing okay. She still tried to look after me.

She tapped a panel at the front of her desk, revealing a small fridge. Grabbing two bottles of Rocket Water, she carried them and the food over to the sitting area.

"How's school?" she asked as we sat.

I stared at her.

"Fine, fine. Tell me about this mystery date of yours." She leaned closer, eyes fixed on me.

I sampled a mushroom. "No mystery. We met at our

advisor's office."

"Who is she? What's she like? Did you ask her out or did she?"

"Briar. She's great. I did."

Cassi groaned. "You're the worst. I'm dying of curiosity and you're being you."

I hid a smile, not wanting to reveal how much I enjoyed messing with her. I was her younger brother, after all. Some things never got old.

"At least tell me she makes you happy."

"She does." That part was true. "You'll like her."

"What's more important is you like her."

"I do." My heart knocked as I said it. Definitely a warning sign. As much as I tried to fight it, I felt the after effects of having her body close to mine.

Cassi nudged more food in my direction. "Poor Eva was devastated."

"Sorry."

"No, it's my fault. I knew you were hiding something from me." She wagged her fork in my direction. "Should've known it was a girl."

I shifted in my seat. What I'd been hiding was that I didn't want to go on any more dates. Still, if she thought Briar was the reason for my reluctance, even better.

"Tell me something about her. Something fun."

"She likes chocolate."

"Okay, you have to at least try."

"She's into sloths. AlterEgo."

"They're coming here in a few weeks. Bring her."

"She'll be thrilled." Least I hoped she would. We hadn't discussed how many dates she'd have to sit through for the deal.

"So you guys will come?"

"Sure." I expected to feel my usual reluctance. The dread

of having to grit my teeth through another forced date.

I didn't. In fact, I was anticipating it. I wanted to see Briar in another dress, sitting in my car. Wanted to feel her body against mine while she swayed to music.

And I didn't want it to end there. I wanted my hands under her dress. On her body.

Warning signs. In fact, I'd moved beyond warning into danger. She'd caught me off guard, with her quick humor, her quirks. Those legs.

I shoved my desires aside for now. Not exactly appropriate when having a conversation with your sister.

Plus, I needed time. Time to get a handle on myself. Once the night was over and Briar and I got started on the project, I'd have less time to think about her legs. We'd buckle down and get to business. Strictly business.

I spent some time catching up with my sister. I gave her the usual about classes and she bemoaned the setbacks she'd experienced.

"It's frustrating!" She used her fork to stab the air as she spoke. "If you say you're going to do something, then do it." She gestured toward the window. "The booth, the lights? All hinging on this contractor who's in the middle of a quarter-life crisis."

I chuckled. "What'd you do?"

"Gave him a piece of my mind and hired someone else. It's hard to find reliable people sometimes." She grinned, rubbed my knee. "I'm lucky to have you and Alba. People I can count on."

"You can always count on me."

"I know."

It hadn't always been that way. After the battle with Landmine, I'd woken in the hospital, my body a mess of broken bones and bandaged wounds.

Cassi had been with me. Curled up in a chair, sobbing into a wad of tissues so she wouldn't wake me.

Never again, I thought.

Cassi's HC chimed. "That'll be the hourly update. You go ahead. I'll be there in a minute. Can't wait to meet your date." Her brows raised and lowered a few times.

I left the lounge, took a moment on the staircase. The wall of music crashed against me. The energy from the crowd was a palpable thing, filling the room.

I headed down the stairs, searching for Briar. She was sitting at the bar, talking to a guy wearing flashy clothes.

As I watched, the guy pushed into her space. She leaned back from him, her expression tight. The guy said something that made her eyes widen.

My hands fisted at my sides. I ground my teeth, cold fury rushing through my blood.

Stalking across the room, I rounded to the bar.

"Hey—" Briar cut off when I slid an arm around her waist. Meeting the guy's furious gaze, I pressed her to my side.

I didn't want to get violent. That's not who I am. Not anymore. It's one of the reasons I keep a tight rein on myself. I knew what I was like when I didn't. Someone ugly and aggressive. Someone who didn't deserve the second chance he'd been given.

Plus, if the other guy throws a punch? Nothing I can't handle.

But seeing that guy get in Briar's face had unleashed the black rage inside me. It churned through my veins, pounded in my skull.

The guy's lips pulled back in a sneer. His shoulders tensed, his chest thrown out.

I watched, waited. I hadn't expected to get into a fight.

But I sure as hell wasn't going to walk away from one.

17 LULLABY

"Hey, babe," Gage said to me, giving me the half-smile I used to love. "You shouldn't have followed me here. It's way fault."

"I didn't. I have a date."

He snorted. "Yeah, right."

The red head glowered at me like I was a lower life form. "I want my drink."

Gage's arm tightened around her neck, drawing her in to nuzzle at her temple.

My stomach tightened. I remembered him doing that to me. Not that I wanted him to do it again. Gage was an asshole, a fact I'd learned the hard way. Still, having him do it to someone else in front of me was disconcerting.

And infuriating. He was showing off, letting me know how much better off he was now that he'd ditched his "boring" ex-girlfriend.

He whispered something in her ear and she giggled before making her way to the opposite side of the bar. I heard her banging on the counter and yelling for service.

Gage turned back to me, sliding his thumbs into the front pocket of his jeans. "What do you want, Briar?"

"I told you," I said through clenched teeth. "I'm here with someone."

"Yeah, okay."

I swallowed back the urge to explain, to insist. Gage was too egotistical to realize the rest of the world didn't revolve around him. He assumed I'd invented a fake date to impress him.

I glanced over the bar. Alba stood at the other end, serving customers. I considered calling for her or a bouncer, but the last thing I wanted was to make a scene. I was supposed to be impressing Jase's sister, not arguing with my toxic ex.

My cheeks burned. The club seemed too dark and too bright at the same time. I wanted nothing more than to be in my apartment, tucked into my bed in my pajamas.

Gage's eyes dragged over my body. "I don't get you. While we're dating, I can't get you to leave the house. Now, you're here, dressed like this."

God, what a jerk. In the beginning, he'd been attentive, affectionate. The cool boyfriend I'd longed for in high school.

I knew why he was pissed. The last time we'd had sex? Things hadn't ended on a high note. He'd dropped all pretenses after. Let his true personality show through.

I wasn't going to play his games. However I also wasn't going to let him get away with slut shaming me.

I tilted my head, crossed my legs. "Guess I never wanted to leave the house when it meant subjecting myself to more of your face."

He flushed a dark red. "Fucked up coming from a tight-ass prude."

I rolled my eyes. One second, I was a slut, the next I was a prude.

Typical asshole. So uncreative.

I dragged the little skewer through the remnants of chocolate foam. Nibbled the tip. "Whatever. Go play your little games with your new girl." I met his eyes, smiled sweetly. "Before I fall asleep talking to you."

Gage bared his teeth, his neck flushing deep red. He moved toward me.

I braced, tapped into my ability. One touch and he'd be out cold. In fact, I hoped he did touch me. Then I'd knock his sorry ass out on the floor.

A strong arm slid around my waist. I looked up as Jase's hand gripped my hip in a firm, possessive gesture.

Jase's dark eyes fixed on Gage, fierce and fixed. Gage glowered back, his hands fisting at his sides. I could practically sense the two of them flexing and snarling while they circled one another.

"Jase," I said quickly, my voice high and tight. "This is Gage, he was just leaving." When neither of them moved, I gave Jase's arm a firm pinch.

He dragged his gaze from Gage to look at me. "You alright?" His voice emerged rough, spoken through gritted teeth. The cool control on his features a stark contrast to the blatant anger on Gage's.

But there was something in Jase's eyes I hadn't seen before. A wild rage tempered by hard focus. It shook me to the core. Went against everything I thought I knew about Jase. He was the smart one, the upstanding one. The honors, straight A, high achiever.

I'd been relieved when he arrived, hoping his appearance would smooth things over. Now, I panicked. This wasn't a man who'd deescalate the situation.

This man was looking for a fight.

"This is what you like?" Gage sneered. "Some pretty boy?"

My pulse raced as I looked from one to the other. "Jase, don't."

He ignored me, his shoulders flexing as he stepped towards Gage.

Shit, shit! Gage was a normie, but he was also a hothead. He wouldn't hesitate to throw a punch, even against a PN.

Plus, I was shaken over what I'd seen in Jase's eyes. A grim fury. I didn't think he'd take advantage over a weaker opponent, but he also wasn't going to let Gage walk away without a scratch.

Scenarios flashed through my head. A fight, injuries, the three of us getting arrested. A black mark from the institute, disciplinary actions. Jase losing his status as a perfect student.

I swallowed, my palms clammy. I couldn't let it happen, not over an asshole like Gage, and not to Jase. Not in his sister's club on opening night. If he got into a fight, it would be my fault.

Gage's hand shot out, grabbing for Jase's collar. Jase slapped his hand away, the move derisive. Both men raised their fists.

Shooting to my feet, I grabbed each of them by the arm, tapping into my ability. Their energies flooded into me, two churning tides of aggressive male wrath.

"Wh—" Gage's eyes rolled into his head. He crumpled to the floor, sprawling on his back.

Jase's arms flexed, his will fighting mine. It was no use. He shot me one dark look before he, too, slid to the floor.

I stood over the two of them, trying to control the sudden influx of energy. It was like having straight caffeine pumping through my blood. My limbs shook, my breath came in short, quick gasps, my lungs squeezing. My heart raced a mile a minute, pounding against my ribs.

The people around us stopped, staring and whispering.

Someone screamed. Bouncers pushed through the crowd, expressions grim as they stalked towards me.

Alba rushed over, eyes wide. "What the hell happened?"

"It's okay!" I raised my voice loud for everyone to hear. "They're not dead!"

18 LULLABY

"Here." Cassi held a can out to me. Rocket Water, grapefruit.

"Thanks." I popped the top, took a deep drink. The crisp, tart flavor washed away the lingering taste of sweet chocolate and liquor.

The three of us, Cassi, Jase, and I, were sitting in Jase's studio apartment. Well, Cassi and I were sitting. Jase was sprawled face down on the bed.

She'd rushed onto the scene at Iceberg and I'd managed to explain what happened. She called over one of the bouncers, had him haul Jase out of the club into the car. We'd ridden over together in what had to be one of the weirdest and most awkward situations of my life.

Cassi glanced at her brother. I'd assured her that he'd be alright, but she was worried. Couldn't blame her. The guy was out cold. In my haste to stop him and Gage, I'd opened the channels far wider than necessary. He'd be down for awhile.

"Sorry for what happened," I said.

Cassi chuckled. "It's not your fault. In fact, you stopped

both of them before they did any damage." She'd watched the video, marking Gage as a future person non grata.

I didn't agree with her. If I hadn't been there, Gage wouldn't have provoked Jase. And Jase, as my fake boyfriend, probably felt obliged to confront him. It became a huge mess with security dumping Gage in a Blackbird, his red head girlfriend screaming at me as they dragged her out.

Now, I was fighting not to squirm while his sister studied me.

Jase's apartment was a sleek studio space, inlaid with dark wood and gleaming tiles. The wall to wall offered an amazing view. The city spread to the horizon beyond, a million lights in the darkness. A wide bed spanned the main area, the covers dark grey.

We sat at the round table in front of the kitchen area. While I sipped, I took in the surroundings. No art, no scattered clothing, no kicked off shoes. Each surface gleamed. It was understated and masculine, much like Jase himself.

"So, you and my brother are dating?" Cassi's brows lifted when I stared at her.

"Yes," I said, forcing a grin. "We just started. And my ex is a real asshole."

"Hey, I get the whole toxic-ex thing. Happens to all of us. Still, I'm glad he brought you."

"He's a great guy."

"He is." She hesitated. "It's first time he's brought someone to meet me."

I swallowed, a cold sweat forming on my skin. I hated lying to Cassi, and talking about Jase while he was in the room made my stomach knot. Even if he was unconscious.

"You should stay the night."

I snapped out of my thoughts. "I should?"

"He's out for the count, and you've been drinking. Even

with an automated ride, I'd feel better if you stayed. You seem kind of shaken."

The concern on her face made the guilt worse. Not to mention, I'd pretty much botched the whole first impression thing. I wanted to make up for it.

"You're right," I said. "I'll watch Jase. Make sure he's okay."

Her expression softened. "Great."

Whew.

"I've got to get back to the club. Help yourself to whatever. Come by Iceburg with your friends. I'll list you as VIP." She paused in the doorway, smiling. "Circumstances aside, I think you'll be good for him. He needs some goodness in his life."

Her words reminded me of Alba's. From what I'd seen, he was doing fine, but maybe I was missing something.

After she'd gone, I leaned against the door for a minute with my eyes closed. Everything caught up with me, leaving me dizzy.

One thing was for sure. I wasn't spending another minute in that dress.

I pulled off my heels and poked around at the wall panels, searching for a closet or a bureau. I prodded at each bump and notch, hesitant to ask the wallscreen for help in case it woke Jase.

I eventually found a drawer under the bed itself. It slid out, revealing neatly folded clothes. Thankfully, Jase had a lot of t-shirts.

My cheeks burned as I slipped out of dress, trying to convince myself it was for necessity. As quietly as possible, I stripped to my underwear and went through a series of exercises to burn through the extra energy. Lunges, bridges, squats. I kept a few Extra Strength Insta-snooze patches in my bag for when I was too charged for exercise to work, but using them left me groggy and nauseous.

By the time I finished, I was sweating and my false lashes were stuck to my cheeks. I peeled them off, showered in the spotless, ultra-modern bathroom, then slipped on the shirt.

As I draped my dress over a chair, I passed a frame displaying rotating images. I smiled at the shots of Jase as a kid, mugging at the camera. Another one showed him as a teen. He'd been lankier then, his frame hinting at the man he'd become. His expression was more closed off. Wary.

All the shots were of him and Cassi. No parents or other relatives.

Cassi said that I was the first person Jase brought to meet her. I'd assumed she'd meant recently or since attending the institute. Maybe she'd meant ever.

I stifled a yawn. The extra energy spiraled out of me and I was crashing hard. The plan was to grab a little sleep, then wake before Jase, get dressed before he saw me in his clothes. Explain what'd happen, say I'd covered with his sister.

Except there was one bed. Not even a couch, and the only chairs were the metal ones at the dining table.

I glanced at Jase. He was so long, so male. And so taking up most of the bed.

I climbed under the covers, did my best to tuck as much blanket between our bodies as I could. His warmth had seeped into the sheets, making the bed a comfy cocoon.

I let my gaze rest on Jase. The strong line of his neck sloping into broad shoulders. His features lost that guarded expression while sleeping. His brow relaxed, mouth soft.

The abrupt change in the club haunted me. Had me questioning all my assumptions about Jase. He'd shut down when I asked about changing his handle. Had tried to turn me away from working with him. Why?

As I drifted to sleep, I wondered what else he was hiding from me.

19 STRONGHOLD

I jerked awake, my eyes snapping open. Bright morning light pierced my head, added to the painful throb behind my temples. I recognized my bed, my apartment. Morning light streamed in, casting everything in pale white.

Including the warm, still form of Briar, tucked against me.

My stomach clutched. We slept together? My pulse pounded against my temples as I watched her chest rise and fall, her full breasts pushing against the front of what I recognized as one of my t-shirts.

I closed my eyes, clawed through the memories of the night before. The club, seeing Cassi. Confronting the asshole. Briar grabbing my arm.

Ah.

I exhaled, let the tension rush out of me. Now that I looked at myself, I was fully dressed in the clothes I'd worn the night before.

I rubbed the back of my neck. It unsettled me seeing Briar in my space. Her golden hair spread across the pillow, her lips slightly parted. There wasn't much room on the bed, and her bare leg lay alongside mine.

She made a soft noise, curling towards me. I tucked the blanket around her, careful not to touch her skin. The urge to put my arm around her, draw her into my warmth, hit me hard.

Instead, I got up, hit the shower. Bracing my hands on the wall, I ducked my head under the spray, my braincells waking. This time, the effects of Briar's ability lasted longer.

I set my jaw. We were going to have to talk about her putting me to sleep again.

As I dumped my clothes in the hamper, pulled on some loose pants, the mirror screen flashed the time. I was usually long awake, running or training. Instead, I was sleeping the day away.

Inexcusable.

When I emerged, Briar was sitting up, pushing her hair out of her face. Her eyes traveled over my bare torso before returning to my face.

"Hey," she said. Her voice was rough from sleep. She appeared soft and mussed, her clean face and tumbled hair a sharp contrast to how she'd been the night before.

"Morning," I said.

"So much for my plan."

"Plan?"

"Nothing." She pressed her mouth in a tight line. "Awkward, huh?"

I went to the kitchen, activated the coffee maker. "Want to tell me what happened?"

"Um, my ex-boyfriend tried to pick a fight with you, so I kind of intervened."

Coffee flowed from the spout, dark and smelling like heaven. I lifted the sugar and cream and when Briar nodded, added both to the mugs.

I carried both back to the bed, offered her one. "And that meant putting us both to sleep."

"Best I could do at the time." She accepted the mug, leaning back against the pillows. She'd said it was awkward, though she seemed comfortable enough. Downright cozy.

I sipped coffee, willed it to chase away the dregs of fatigue. "The asshole?"

"Cassi threw him out. She said he'd be banned from every club on the east coast."

"She's got a low tolerance for assholes." I leaned closer, waited for her to look at me. "Want to talk about it?" Weird, asking your fake girlfriend about her ex. But the look on Briar's face pulled at me.

She fidgeted with the blankets. "Sometimes when I'm stressed, I lose my grip on my powers."

"Growing pains" weren't uncommon. The teens and early twenties years were tough for PNs. Most of us were still settling into our powers.

"Gage and I dated my freshman year. I was new at everything, trying to get a grip on my abilities, on being at the institute. I was so focused on not draining others I didn't realize I was doing the opposite. Letting some of my energy slip into them."

She toyed with her mug. "Once, he was going down on me and I overcompensated. I fell asleep. Snoring and everything."

I coughed, set my coffee down.

Briar groaned. "I know! Even when I explained, he never got over it. His real colors came through after that."

She put her mug aside. "Anyway, it's over now."

If I ever saw that guy again, I'd make double sure of it.

Out loud, I said, "By the time my sister's done with him, he won't be able to get into an outhouse without getting thrown out."

Briar laughed. "Sorry about what happened."

"Nothing happened. Thanks to you."

"Your sister said the same thing. Still, it made a commotion on opening night."

"Probably be good for business." I took her cup, set it and mine on the table. "You're not responsible for his actions."

She exhaled. "Okay."

"I get why you did it, but I'm going to ask you not to drain me again." I hated the idea of being unable to move, to defend. Helpless.

"Promise. Just didn't want you guys to bust the furniture."

"Could've taken him in my—"

Her pillow hit me in the face. "Do not say it!"

I pushed the pillow back at her. "What's wrong, Zee?"

"How dare you call me that."

I leaned in, whispered in her ear. "Zee."

She climbed to her knees, laughing as she shoved the pillow into my face. I hooked an arm around her waist, flipped her over. Her hair brushed against me and I caught a whiff of my shampoo, my soap, combining with the scent of her skin.

She yelped as she landed on her back, sprawled over the covers. Her grin faded as I braced myself over her, my hands splayed on either side of her head. She held her breath, my shirt sinking between the valley of her breasts.

"You're gorgeous." My voice came out rough.

Her cheeks turned pink. Her eyes roamed over me. Hungry. "You're one to talk." Her hand lifted, hovered. She hesitated, sent me a questioning glance.

"Go ahead."

She spread her palm over my chest. Her soft, warm fingers explored my torso. Traveling over my shoulders and arms. Down my abs. Brushed over my obvious erection. She bit her lip, fingers skimming me through my pants.

I fought for control even as my blood roared. "Careful."

"Trying to be a gentleman again?"

I lowered myself enough to drink in her scent. "You make it tough."

"Then stop."

She surged up, her lips crashing against mine. The contact rocked me, sent a spike of pure lust thundering through me.

I hooked my arms around her waist, letting my weight press her to the bed. Her arms banded around my neck, her lips parting against mine. The promises I'd made to myself about control, about keeping my head in the game, shattered.

There was only Briar, here, willing. In my arms.

The kiss turned blistering, her mouth warm and eager and wet. She moaned against my mouth and I drank in the sound.

Our bodies molded together, her thighs cradling my hips. I rocked against her, thrilled when she arched against me. Her hands roamed my back, demanding I come closer. I gripped the outside of her thigh, curled her leg around my waist. Ground against her.

She gasped as I sank my teeth into her neck. "Jase."

What thin strands of control I had left snapped. I grabbed the bottom of the shirt, dragged it up to expose her body. I gathered her nipple into my mouth, drew on it until she gasped.

"Gorgeous," I said, kissing my way down her body until I reached the place between her legs. Found her hot, wet. Eager for my tongue. I wasn't ready to be inside her. Not yet.

But I had to make her come. Needed to watch her lose control.

Shifting, I lay alongside her, grabbed both her wrists. I brought them over her head, used one hand to hold them to the bed. My other hand skimmed over her body, cupped her.

She gasped as my fingers explored her soft, slick folds. Her eyes closed as I rubbed my forefinger over her clit.

"Here?" I watched her, the way her head fell back and her breath hitched. I adjusted my touch. "Or here?"

"Right there. God, don't stop." She writhed, ground against my palm. Cried out when I slid two fingers into her.

My fingers buried deep, I used my thumb to pleasure her, rubbing in small, controlled circles. She writhed, her sex pulsing around my fingers. My other hand gripped her wrists, keeping her arms over her head.

"Jase," she panted. She grew hotter, wetter, squeezing around my fingers. Her features flushed red, her feet digging into the covers.

"Come for me."

She did. Her legs shot out straight, the muscles in her thighs and calves tensing. She let out a keening cry, her brows drawn together, lips parted as she rode out the pleasure.

I drew my fingers from her and, while she watched, slid them into my mouth. Savored the taste of her. I wanted more. Wanted to bury myself to the hilt in her tight, wet heat. Wanted those sexy little cries ringing in my ears and those tantalizing nipples in my mouth.

Moving up the bed, I gathered her against me, pulled the covers over her.

"What about you?" she asked, her voice a little rough.

"Just come here."

She snuggled in, her arm thrown over my chest, her leg over mine. Her mouth curved in a little smile. She made a soft sound, like a contented cat.

Within seconds, she was asleep.

I kept her tucked against me while I stared at the ceiling, wondering what the hell we were doing.

20 LULLABY

"And your supervisor says your work is exemplary." Dr. Singh nodded as she scanned the report. "You're their most requested mentor."

"Thank you. The new candidates are an impressive group."

I was sitting in Dr. Singh's office, my screen in front of me while I made notes. It'd been a couple of weeks since Jase and I visited his sister's club. Since then, we'd met on alternating days to work on the project. We kept our meetings at Jubilee's, both of us making the silent agreement to stay in public places.

Outside the office, the faculty wing bustled with activity. The teleporting guy appeared for a blink, dropped a packet on the corner of Dr. Singh's desk, then was gone again. Someone's HC beeped.

"We'll need them." Dr. Singh's eyes glittered. "Our west coast cohorts swept us in the debate championships but they are not stealing the Robopalooza win this year."

I swallowed a laugh. If the students were competitive, the faculty could be downright bloodthirsty.

Dr. Singh's expression tightened. Instead of her usual offer of black tea, her greeting had been a harried nod and an apology while she flicked through her screen searching for my file.

"Is everything alright?" I asked.

"I'm running behind." She pushed at her hair. "Ashley didn't come in to work today. Apparently there was a last minute volunteer opportunity at Osprey Beach Park It's left me in a lurch."

"Need help?" Superhero. Had to offer.

"Thank you, but you focus on your candidacy." Her features brightened. "Speaking of which, how is the project going?"

My cheeks burned. Did having a searing petting session count as progress? I gave her a quick outline of what we'd worked on.

"It's a good direction. An excellent one."

"Really?" I perked at the praise.

"Absolutely. Resources for PNs are sometimes overlooked. It's important we address those gaps."

Understandable. PNs are impressive. If the extra strength, stamina, and fast healing didn't make it obvious, science and medicine are a little more fluid for us. In addition to our abilities, we're also more hearty. We're quick to react, tough in a fight, fast to heal.

But I knew first hand not all wounds are superficial. Not all damage is physical

"Let's generate a resource list. See what research has already been done." Dr. Singh tapped at her screen, sent me links for articles. "When I designed the program, I knew you and Jase would be perfect candidates. The board is sure to approve the program for open application once they hear your thesis."

My stomach twisted. Jase and I were walking a thin line.

Especially after what'd happened at his place. Had it been a one time deal or was there something more?

The questions crowded my mind while I worked my shift at the resource center. I made a ton of small errors, exasperating both myself and the first years I was attempting to help.

I jabbed at the HC screen in front of me. It flashed red, informing me I'd entered the wrong password too many times in a row and now it was locked.

Victoria's elbow knocked against mine. "What's with you? In the break room, you added poultry seasoning to your coffee."

"I thought it was cinnamon." I covered my face with my hands. "Hawthorne's going to kill me."

"No, he'll just leave you out for the birds so your bleached skull can act as a warning to his enemies. Speak of the devil."

Hawthorne cruised into the room, long and lean, his sweater a creamy white against his deep, cool brown skin. A pair of thick black glasses framed his brown eyes, his dark hair close cropped.

He stopped when he noticed my screen. "Briar."

"Boss. The machines turned against me."

He narrowed his eyes, used his administration code to unlock and restart my screen.

Victoria leaned in after he left. "We should add poultry seasoning to his fancy tea."

"No! Well. No." I shook my head. "Definitely not."

"Tell me what's going on. Although it's fun watching you have a meltdown. You're usually—"

"I fooled around with someone and now I don't know where we stand." It came out in one long rush.

"Ah, buyer's remorse."

"He's not a pair of shoes I got on clearance."

"Not so different. The question is, what do you do now? Tell yourself lesson learned or do you keep it in your closet out of some twisted sense of obligation until, five years down the road, you finally throw them into the donation bin?"

"I have no idea what you're saying."

"The point is, don't leave the shoes in the trunk of a car. Either take them out and enjoy them, or find the receipt and return them."

As my afternoon Preternaturals in Politics class dragged on, I mulled over her advice. Victoria wasn't wrong. The smart thing would be to write it off. He'd said plain as day he didn't want a relationship.

How was I supposed to forget the way his lips devoured mine in that bruising kiss? The fierce attention he'd paid while bringing me to searing peak. The sweet cuddling after.

When I'd woken, Jase was fully dressed, standing in front of the window. My smile faded when I saw the grim expression on his face.

It stung. I'd gotten a glimpse of his humor and passion only to have it snatched away.

The drive home had been tense. None of the easy friendliness we'd shared, no sense of the intimacy that'd burned through us moments earlier. Just Jase's measured silence and my own discomfort.

Our meetings since been purely business. We discussed the project, combed the research, debated various points. I kept finding myself distracted by small things. Our fingers brushed, our knees bumped under the table. It brought me back to being touched, his mouth hot and hungry on mine.

When we weren't ignoring the raw lust between us, the two of us got along great. As reluctant as he'd been to sign on, Jase never slouched or cruised through his share of the work. We debating articles, exchanged ideas, fleshed out concepts. Sexual tension aside, we made good partners.

My HC chirped, drawing me back to the present. The message made me grimace. "Damn."

"Bad news?" Victoria asked.

"The worst," I muttered. "Fancy cocktail party."

21 LULLABY

For the second time in one month, I was in a fancy dress in fancy surroundings. This time, I couldn't hang out and listen to music while drinking. I had to make conversation.

With people. Fancy people.

The upscale lounge sprawled over Iceburg's rooftop, a pristine oasis of plush sofas, ottomans, and low tables. The city stretched into the distance, infinite bright lights against the indigo sunset sky. Floating orb lights bobbed in the air like tiny fairies, drifting on an unseen current. Music hummed in the background, low-key and electronic. The late September air was breezy and balmy.

Guests clustered in small groups, speaking in low voices as they sampled cocktails and minuscule appetizers. Celebrities, musicians, and one woman I recognized from "Hero Wives." Jewelry sparked against throats, winked from wrists, dangled from ears.

Jase exchanged greetings with a light-skinned blonde woman wearing a pristine purple suit. Her date, a tall woman with warm brown skin and long braids, stood next to her.

"This is Briar Williams," he said. "She's a license candidate with me at the institute. This is Mayor Reynolds."

"Former Mayor," said Reynolds. "This is Eva Brysons. She designs and models for Maison Écarlate."

"You must be impressive to keep up with the Parks," Eva said in a soft French accent.

I managed a choked laugh. "Oh, he's impressive enough for the both of us."

Former Mayor Reynolds smiled. "Are the two of you attending next month's fundraiser?"

"Wouldn't miss it." Shoot, what fundraiser?

After a few more pleasantries, the two of them moved on. Jase lowered his head to murmur in my ear. "Nervous?"

"A little." I reached for confidence. I didn't want Jase to babysit me. This was my part of the bargain to hold up. "Did you tell me about a fundraiser?"

"There's always one happening."

"Hey, you two." Looking sharp in black pants and a ruffled mauve blouse, Cassi held out two cocktails. "Enjoying yourselves?"

"A blast." I clutched the glass, glad for something to hold.

"I hope my brother's taking good care of you."

I slipped my arm around Jase's, squeezed his hand. "He's a great boyfriend."

Cassi brightened. "Isn't he too quiet? What do you like best about him?"

"Sis." Jase sighed.

She laughed. "Sorry, big sister mode. What about you, Jase? What drew you to Briar?"

"She smart and she works hard. She's easy to talk to, reliable. And she's funny."

Heat crept up my neck. Was any of it true or was all of it for show?

Alba joined us, her arm sliding around Cassi's middle. Watching the two of them gave me a pang of envy. How nice to be with someone, knowing they liked you back.

I finished my cocktail, let it soothe the bitterness in my throat. The two of them moved off and Jase's palm rested against my lower back as he guided me closer to the railing. We gazed over the city, the sounds of the party quiet behind us.

"You alright?" Jase asked after awhile. "You seem uncomfortable."

I fumbled for a response. How to tell your fake boyfriend you might be falling for him? "I'm not used to lying."

"Sorry to force you."

"Hey, no one's forcing anything. Maybe I'll get good at it. Then I can take on undercover work. Become a secret agent."

He chuckled. "Sure."

"You doubt me."

"You're too nice."

"It doesn't sound like a compliment."

"It is." His fingers skimmed up my bare arm to the side of my neck. He brushed back my hair from my shoulder, the contact sending chills through my skin. "It's you."

"What's with the sweet talk?"

"I'm not sure," he admitted. "But you're fine the way you are."

I swallowed, my pulse pounding. In my heels, I could kiss him if I rose up a little. Especially if I grabbed him by the collar, pulled him down to meet me. A starry night, a rooftop kiss. Beyond romantic.

Would he let me? And if he did, would it be because he wanted to kiss me or because he wanted to fool his sister?

My HC pinged, startling me. Jase's went off at the same time, the sounds identical.

Jase grimaced. "Field exercises."

"Right when things were getting good," I muttered, turning off the signal.

"What?"

"Nothing."

"I'll tell Cassi we're leaving."

I decided to change in the bathrooms instead of in the car. In the stall, as I struggled to get out of my dress and into my bodysuit, I also took the opportunity to compose myself.

What had I been thinking? Picturing the two of us as sweethearts. Getting caught up in my own little fantasies. I couldn't keep doing that to myself. It was only going to make me miserable.

Someone tapped on the door. "Hey, it's Alba. Pass me your dress?"

"Thanks." I threw it over the top of the door.

"We'll send it over to you, dry-cleaned."

"I appreciate it." I threw my hair into a ponytail, exited the stall.

Alba had my dress over her arm. She studied me for a moment, head tilted. "You and Jase. I was suspicious last time, now I'm sure of it. Something's going on between you two."

"Well, we are dating."

"You're not manipulating him?"

I stiffened, hands fisting. "He's with me out of his own free will." Not exactly a lie. Still, my insides knotted.

Alba frowned. "I like you, and I hope you're telling the truth. Because I'm not going to let anyone hurt Cassi or her brother. They've been through enough."

"What do you mean?"

"It's not for me to say, and if Jase hasn't told you, he doesn't want you to know."

The words stuck with me on the ride back to the institute.

No matter how much I told myself our relationship wasn't real, it hurt knowing Jase didn't trust me.

Worse was realizing how much I wanted him to trust me. To give me more than just a glimpse of the real him.

I debated telling him about Alba's suspicions. In the end, I kept it to myself. If Alba was suspicious, it had to be my fault for being a poor liar.

My uncle was right. I needed to toughen up. Get my head in the game.

We arrived back at the institute and hurried over to the fields. Stadium lights lit up the space, drops of dew glittering on the grassy lawn. Dozens of other candidates moved towards the sign in area or went through warm ups.

A group of guys arrived without shirts, half their bodies painted bright blue. They rushed to sign in, wipe the paint, and change into bodysuits. Exercises were random. Dead of night, stormy weather, in the middle of class. The idea was to make us drop everything and report to the exercise area within a certain time frame. Practice for when we became licensed and began responding to emergency situations.

"You're on front line?" I asked Jase.

"Squad leader."

Of course. "I'm on the support team." I hesitated, then added, "Good luck out there."

I hurried off, my face growing hot. In truth, I'd wanted to kiss him. The exercises were dangerous. Brutal, even. Designed to test us to our utmost limits. Injuries, dire ones, weren't uncommon.

Head in the game, I reminded myself. If anyone could take care of himself, it was Jase. I had my own duties to worry about.

I rushed into the support sign up area, gave my name and student ID. Victoria stood ripping open packets of nutrient bars. "Hey, welcome to the party."

"I just left one, actually."

"Pity. Here." She tossed me a nutrient bar.

In the tent, the support squad rushed to prep. Setting up rest areas, preparing provisions, checking supplies. Dr. Linden was overseeing the activity, though he gave no orders or directions. We were supposed to make decisions on our own, think on our feet.

His screen was open and occasionally he made notes, probably about our performance. Catching my eye, he gave me a grin and a thumbs up.

I got to work, chewing my way through the bar and tucking another one into my belt.

Victoria gasped, pointed at the sky. "Oh my God, it's her. Archangel."

Breath catching, I looked up.

A figure soared through the air, her suit royal blue and matte gold against amber-colored skin. Around us, the other support squad candidates stopped to gawk. The front line squads did the same, chins tipped up, eyes fixed on the sky.

She slowed, then came to a perfect landing near the end of the field. Her hair, a deep brown fading to auburn near the ends, swung from a high ponytail as she joined the cluster of professors.

"Wow, a real war hero," Victoria whispered. "Think she'd take a selfie with me?"

"She's so beyond," I murmured, unable to tear my eyes away. Flying was one of the rarest abilities, a top tier power. Knowing she'd seen action during the St. John's River Battle made her even more awe-inducing.

Behind us, Dr. Linden cleared his throat, raised an eyebrow at us.

We scurried back to work, moving faster than before, our expressions determined.

If a veteran was observing, it meant the exercise was going to be intense. We needed to be ready for anything.

22 STRONGHOLD

W hen I signed on for the crisis and disaster track, one of the first things they drilled into us was energy management.

"The key," the instructor told us. "Is to channel your abilities where they're most needed. Use your energy efficiently. A lot of adrenaline flowing, a lot of instinct to react. But remember, our energies aren't infinite. Pause and plan."

I mulled over the words as I signed in, the screen changing over to a list of potential squad members. As a leader, I had a chance to pick two teammates, with the final randomly assigned. Sometimes I chose all random, a chance to work with different PNs with varying abilities.

Tonight, I scrolled the list, found two names I trusted. A veteran was observing. I wasn't going to give less than my A game. I marked the names, let the last slot fill in with a random.

The balmy night air was calm and quiet. For the moment. Palpable tension ran through the candidates, the arrival of the Archangel upping the stakes.

On the perimeter, support tents stood stark white against

the evening sky. Lights cast bright glows against the darkness, illuminating the tent interiors.

I searched for Briar. Being in the support squad didn't make you immune to attack. I'd seen the tents be overrun, the PNs inside taking heavy damage.

I raked a hand through my hair. What the hell was wrong with me? Briar was a Powerhouse. She could take care of herself.

Why the fierce desire to protect her?

Hector flashed into existence beside me. "What's up, Park? Something wrong?"

"Forget it," I muttered. Putting Briar out of my head, I moved through a series of warm up exercises until my head cleared and my limbs loosened.

Around us, other combat PNs did the same. A Chinese-American woman, her hair dyed honey blonde, jogged past. Fingerless fighter's gloves in bright pink encased her hands. Probably a speedster. They were into fighting as close to barehanded as possible.

Hector bounced on his toes, stretched. "Who else did you pick?"

"Here she comes." I watched as a short woman with olive-toned skin and chin-length brown hair jogged up to us.

"Always a fun time with you guys." She knocked fists with Hector, turned to me to do the same.

"Serena. Good to see you back on your feet."

"Barely a scratch."

Her "scratch" had been a broken rib and a fractured arm. Despite her overeagerness in a fight, Serena had the strength, the combat skills, and the stamina to deal with whatever the instructors threw at us.

She gestured to the guy beside her. "Found our fourth, too."

The guy was huge, a head taller than me, encased in a

matte black uniform. Everything about him was pale, from his skin to his eyes to his hair. His handle was the same as his first name, "Tristan."

"Welcome to the team," I said, shaking his hand.

Serena grinned. "He's a transfer from the west coast."

Hector whistled, his brows raised. Many considered the west coast university our only rivals in the world, certainly in the U.S. Transfers were almost unheard of.

I decided to see how it played. "Watch each other's backs," I said. "Most important, know your—"

"Limits," Hector and Serena said at the same time.

The signal sounded for us to gather.

A group of professors wearing vivid red and silver made a circle on one end of the field. Light sparked and snapped as they raised their hands, a circle forming above them in midair. Lightening cracked against the sky, snaking out from the portal as it grew.

Mystics. Not as rare an ability as some, but probably the least understood. Something about aether and manipulating the matter of the universe. They were an insular group, following their own rules and curriculum. I'd only ever seen them when they were fabricating monsters to test students.

It was never the same thing twice. Sandworms the size of subway trains with leech mouths. Flying octopuses with acidic ink. Fire-breathing armored robot dinosaurs.

Bugs were the worst. Smaller, easier to kill. But their strength came in their overwhelming numbers.

These were definitely bugs.

The size of terriers, they were spider-like, except with way too many legs and joints. They made me think of a pair of hands joined at the wrists, with extra knuckles.

They poured out of the fissure, mucous-colored skin

glistening. Two yellow orbs bulged from the top of their bodies, each with two watery pupils.

The first shrieking cry rang through the air, a high squeal like metal on glass.

Some of the other teams were given the signal, moved out. Shouts, commands, the sound of abilities activating filled the air, growing to a roar. The speedster with pink gloves crashed into the front ranks, fast and fearless.

I reached for my ability, felt it come alive under my skin.

We got the signal. "Go!" I bellowed.

My team surged forward, plowing into the oncoming wave. A bug swarmed to me, front legs parting to reveal a clasping little mouth. Spittle flew as it clacked rows of tiny pointed teeth.

I grabbed it by the face, my invulnerability flaring to life to harden my skin against the bug's teeth. I squeezed, crushing its head. I flung the body into another, sending it tumbling over backwards.

Hector flashed in and out, popping in to kill a bug before disappearing again. Serena whooped as she leaped, her jump carrying her ten stories into the sky before she crashed into the hoard, sending bug bodies flying.

A bug launched itself at me, legs extended. I braced.

An enormous blade sliced through the air, cutting the bug in half. Tristan loomed, encased in gleaming silver-white armor. Jagged spikes curving out from the shoulders, the gauntlets. He gripped a monstrous ephemeral sword, the same shining silver, and the size of a surfboard.

Both the sword and his armor were bleeding. Thick, old blood oozed from the armor joints, from the edge of the sword, running in red rivers.

A cry of rage drew my attention. Bugs were swarming Serena's feet and ankles, their sheer weight and numbers causing her to buckle. She went down on one knee, teeth gritted as she smashed her fists into the swarm.

"Hector!"

He popped into existence, covered in bug mulch. "Here."

"Draw them off." When he popped out, I turned to Tristan. "Drive them back."

We exchanged nods before throwing ourselves back into the fray.

Other teams surged in and out of my field of vision. Battlecries, explosions, screams of pain. The ground was a ruin of churned earth and dead bugs.

I lost track of time, forgot everything except the fight. There was only the endless wave of my enemies, the satisfying smash of my fists into their bodies. The thrill of losing myself in the rush of battle.

Something grabbed my shoulder. I spun, fist raised.

Hector held up his hands. "It's me!"

I checked my swing, lowered my fist. Realized it was shaking.

He nodded to the signal station.

I looked, chest heaving. We were being pulled back for a respite.

23 STRONGHOLD

I growled, wanting to throw myself back into the fight. Wanted to slam my fists into bodies, feel the crush of monsters. My pulse roared, a constant cadence in my head.

Hector glanced at my hands. I did the same, saw the blood. Beneath the suit's gloves, my skin had broken.

The well was running dry.

I checked the others. Serena roared as she destroyed anything that came her way. Tristan cut through the enemy, silent and steady as a turbine.

I nodded to Hector. "Pull them back."

He vanished, reappeared down the field. I heard Serena arguing. Scowling, she took another leap, landed next to me. "I could go longer."

"I know."

She crossed her arms. "As long as you know it."

Tristan stood nearby. The sword and armor vanished, leaving him in his black bodysuit.

"Reprieve," I said.

We retreated to the recovery tent along with the other

teams who'd been pulled. The exhaustion hit me. My muscles shook with adrenaline and fatigue. Sweat streamed down my temples, coating the back of my neck.

Plus I was freezing, my heightened metabolism eating away at my body's stores. My pulse was sluggish. My head pounded. All signs I'd pushed myself too far.

Know your limits. A hard rule for any PN. We were superheroes with special abilities. Born to save, to fight.

Every time we tapped into our powers, it put an astronomical demand on our bodies. We were like hummingbirds, consuming and expending huge amounts of energy. Without food, rest, recovery, we'd go torpid. Our bodies would collapse, our minds shut down. We'd drop into comas. Or death

I peeled off my gloves, stared at my shaking fingers. If I pushed myself too hard, I'd not only lose my invincibility for a time, I'd be even more prone to injury than a non-PN. My bones would turn brittle, my skin too soft to withstand the barest touch. I'd be like a sand sculpture, ready to crumble at the slightest pressure.

I'd lost myself in the thick of battle. It was my job to keep an eye out for signals. Mistakes like that could cost battles. Lives.

I glanced over at the professors. What had they seen in me? What had the Archangel thought of my performance?

I fisted my hands. I was supposed to be watching over my team, making sure they stayed safe. If Hector hadn't—

"Here." A bottle of sports drink appeared in front of me. Briar stood there, holding nutrient bars. "Want one?"

I drank, the liquid a balm to my dry throat. Briar's lids drooped, her eyes darkly shadowed. She looked pale, hollowed out. "What are you doing?"

"Bolstering the troops. I'm like a walking caffeine hit. Let me show you." She reached for my arm.

Realization hit me. Briar could draw energy out of others. It made sense she could also reverse the energy flow.

She, meanwhile, bore the brunt of that fatigue.

I clenched my jaw. I didn't like that she had to shoulder the weight. She had to be exhausted.

I'd never felt guilty about accepting healing powers before. We were in this together, showing our potential, our dedication.

Briar was different.

I snatched my arm away. "Don't use your powers on me." The words came out hard. Tight.

"Fine. At least take the bar." She shoved one at me. Her lips pressed so hard together they turned bloodless.

"Dammit." I reached out, grabbed her upper arms. She drew in one sharp gasp before I pulled her to me.

I crushed her against my chest, fighting the urge to kiss her until her fatigue drained away. "I hate seeing you like this." A lousy excuse, but it's what I had.

She relaxed against me. Her palms stroked up my back. "I'm tough. I can handle it."

"Yeah. You are." I eased back. "Sorry for being a dick."

"Accepted. You're squishing the food."

I breathed in the scent of her hair. "Good. Peanut butter is the worst one."

"The chocolate chip is the best. Those things are almost good, for nutrient bars." She passed me a lemon bar and hefted a medical kit. "Let me patch you up. You want an Insta-snooze?"

"No, thanks." Sleep was a good way to recover. But using a patch was like being tranquilized. I'd be out cold. I wanted to stay awake and aware.

I ate, let her sterilize and bandage my raw knuckles. Her touch gentle, her movements confident.

"Hey, Park." Serena peeled a nutrient bar as she approached. "Good work out there."

"Same." At Briar's curious gaze, I said, "Briar, Serena. Serena's one of my squad mates."

"We're in the same sociology class," Briar said.

"Sure." Serena chewed her cinnamon bar. "How long you guys been dating?"

"We're not," I said. At the same time, Briar said, "A month."

Serena's brows lifted. "Uh huh."

After she left, Briar gave me a wry look. "We're going to have to work on that."

I shifted in my seat, remembering what passed between us the night of the club opening. The weeks since then had been agonizing. Seeing her and not touching her. Listening to her talk without kissing her. I prided myself on my control, my discipline.

Ever since I'd met Briar, that control was slipping away.

Another signal sounded. The exercise was ending. The mystics closed the portal, using their abilities to clean the aftermath, turning the bug remains back into the stuff of the universe. Soon, our scores would be sent to our accounts, showing us how we'd performed both in our groups and individually.

Briar stretched. "Thank goodness."

"Let me take you home," I said.

She hesitated, then nodded. "Okay. If you come inside." She snapped her medical kit closed, smiled. "I've got killer post-FE snacks."

I walked over to where my teammates waited to sign out. "Good work out there," I said.

"Go team." Hector held a fist out to Tristan. The big guy's expression didn't change, but he returned the bump.

Thinking about his recent transfer, I offered to exchange contact info with him.

"Need a ride?" I asked Hector when the other two left.

"And be the third wheel? Not a chance." He grinned before jogging off.

I scrubbed a hand over my face. Wondered what the hell I was going to do about this.

Because I wasn't sure how much longer I could pretend my feelings towards Briar were just business.

24 LULLABY

I tried to stay awake. Blinked hard, queued music, skimmed notes from class. In the end, the exhaustion took over.

I woke to Jase rubbing my arm. "We're here," he said.

I stretched, pushed my hair out of my face. Realized I was looking up at the car ceiling. "You lowered my seat?"

"Seemed more comfortable."

The gesture warmed me. I swallowed, my throat bone dry. Which meant I'd probably been asleep with my mouth open. Great.

"We were supposed to talk on the way home," I said.

"There's time. You're exhausted."

"So are you. Come inside for a little while. You can shower. Eat something that isn't a packaged mockery of food." I didn't want us to end the day without talking to each other.

Plus, I wanted to check his injuries. The memory of his torn and bloody knuckles shook me. I was used to thinking of Jase as invincible. Impervious.

Seeing his wounds reminded me. He may have been powerful, but he was human.

We climbed onto the curb in front of my building. Jase grabbed the black backpack he always carried with him, signaling the car to go park itself. The streets were quiet, the only sound the rustle of wind through the palm trees.

Our boots clacked against the marble floor of the lobby. "Elevators are our place," I said as I pressed the button.

His mouth curved. "Romantic." His hair was wild and wind blown, the shape of his body clear inside the jumpsuit.

And what a body. He'd seen all of me. Tasted me. It seemed unfair I hadn't gotten the same opportunity.

The doors pinged open. The lights turned on, revealing a quiet, empty condo. I asked the screen if anyone was home.

"Williams, Briar, and one guest."

Alone with my off-limits project partner. Perfect.

While he borrowed my shower, I sent off a quick message to my roommates.

LULLABY: Where did y'all go?
PURLOIN: Study group
INCOGNITO: Work
LULLABY: Jase is here
INCOGNITO: Ooooooooooh
PURLOIN: IIIP? ;)

My cheeks burned. "Implant is in place?" Almost everyone got implanted birth control these days. The insinuation, of course, was that I'd be having sex with Jase.

I ran across the condo to the other shower. I stripped out of my uniform, stepped under the spray. The water sluiced over my body, enveloping me in luscious heat. Nothing like fighting off mystically manifested monsters to make a girl appreciate the little things.

I threw on pajamas, dug up our first aid kit.

Jase emerged, wearing a pair of dark jeans and a soft forest green shirt. His feet were bare, giving him an unguarded appearance. Drops of water fell from the tips of his hair, leaving wet spots on his shirt.

"Thanks for the shower," he said.

I hefted the kit. "How are your hands?"

"Barely scratched."

"Let me see."

He dutifully put his palms on the kitchen counter. I sat on a stool, dabbed at the abrasions with antibiotic cream.

He looked me over, lingering on my wet hair. "No sloths tonight?"

"Got something against penguins?"

He kept a straight face. "A penguin killed my wife."

I burst out laughing, accidentally squeezed the tube too hard. Antibiotic gunk oozed over the back of Jase's knuckles.

"I'm not that injured." He smiled.

I recovered, cleared my throat. "I don't want to cross any lines with you," I said, wiping the mess.

"I think I'm the one who did. At my place."

"I wasn't unwilling. Opposite, actually."

"Not the point."

"Things got kind of heated. We'll find the receipt and return them. Shit, wait. What I mean is, we'll take a step back. You like cookies?" I was avoiding the topic, but I wasn't sure what I wanted for myself and Jase. I needed a moment.

Luckily, Jase seemed as reluctant to discuss matters. He handled the tea while I uncapped one of the enormous storage jars Lucie kept full of her homemade cookies.

We carried our snacks to my room. He stood for a moment,

studying my decor. The lights came to life, casting the room in a warm glow. The diffuser kicked out the soothing scent of lavender vanilla while the wallscreen poured out the gentle sound of rain.

"Make yourself comfortable," I said as we set the snacks and drinks on my desk.

"Impossible to be uncomfortable in here." He took a seat on the edge of the bed, picking up and holding one of the fluffy throw pillows. It looked like he was holding a tiny fuzzy animal.

My heart clutched at the sight of him, all big and manly, surrounded by my blankets and cushions. I wanted to crawl into his lap and insist he pet me.

"Everything's so soft," he said. He sounded amazed.

"Try these. Chocolate cinnamon spiced. They're moan-inducing."

He took a bite. His brows lifted.

"Going to moan?"

"I refuse." He did finish the cookie, though.

I sipped the tea, let it soothe my throat. "God, that's good. I always crash after FEs. When I wake, I'm keyed up and starving."

"So, cookies and tea."

"Or cake and coffee. Mac and cheese and beer." I dipped a cookie into the tea, let it get good and soggy. The subtle taste of cocoa powder, spiked with plenty of cinnamon, washed down with strong tea. Delicious. "What about you? Favorite midnight snack."

"Not much of a night eater."

I nudged him with my elbow.

He paused for a moment, staring at his tea. "My sister would sometimes cook pajeon. Fried green onion pancakes. She'd fry them up, brown and crisp. We'd eat stacks of them."

"Sounds yummy."

His gaze lowered to the floor, his voice quieting. "Been awhile since I thought about them."

My chest squeezed. He sounded sad. Lonely.

I set aside our snacks. "Okay, time for a break."

"That's what we're doing."

"We rested our bodies. Time to rest our brains." I went to the wallscreen, booted my favorite racing game. I activated the holo-controllers, offered him one. "Don't make me use it."

"What?"

"The classic, 'Unless you're afraid you'll lose,' line."

He grabbed the controller. "Loser has to markup an extra article for the project."

I grinned. "You're on."

25 STRONGHOLD

I let myself sink into a world of racing and absurd power ups. Briar and I made increasingly ridiculous rules for each other. Driving backwards, least favorite characters. The entire time, we were settled side by side against a mountain of pillows.

Her ankles tangled with mine. Sometimes I'd rub my foot against hers, tickling her as a distraction. And because I loved the sound of her laugh.

I tossed the controller in defeat. "You're unbeatable."

"I play a lot."

"You're a pro and you didn't even go easy on me." I rolled over onto my side, elbow on the pillows, head propped against my hand.

Briar nestled against me, her head falling against my shoulder. She was a snuggler. Burrowing against me, seeking contact in a dozen small ways. The screen reverted to rain mode, the gentle sound of it making me want to sink into the blankets. I couldn't remember the last time I'd been that relaxed.

Briar made it easy. She made me feel welcome. At home.

"We're supposed to be talking," I said.

"Friendly competition is an excellent form of communication." When I stared, she grimaced. "I know what you're going to say. That we should go back to being partners."

My jaw tightened. I wasn't going to insult her by asking if we could be friends. Not when I wanted to push her down into the mountain of pillows. Kiss her until her eyes went dreamy and those gorgeous thighs wrapped around my hips. "It's for the best."

"Fuck that." Her brows furrowed, blue eyes blazing. "That's the kind of self-sacrificing martyrdom I hate."

"You have no idea."

"Because you won't tell me."

"Then I'll make it clear." I leaned over her until she lay on her back, braced my palms on either side of her head. Her hair spilled on the pillows, her pink lips parting as she stared up at me.

Grabbing her hand, I lifted it to my mouth. Nipped at her fingertips, pressed a kiss to her warm, soft palm. "I can't be around you without wanting my hands on you. I want to feel you around me. Hot and wet. So turned on you can't think straight."

Her breath quickened as I nibbled my way along her arm, found the place where her neck met her shoulder. She shuddered, her head angling as I kissed and and sucked.

Her eyes widened when I wrapped our joined hands around my erection. "This is what you do to me. I want you in every way."

She swallowed, her eyes roving over my body. "I want you, too, Jase." Her fingers streaked up my chest, tangled in my hair. She pulled me down until our mouths met in a hot slap of lips and tongue.

It wasn't enough. I yanked down her pants, shoved her top

up to expose her breasts. I cupped them, teased her nipples. Moved lower, biting her lower stomach, her hip, settled between her legs.

Last time, I'd taken a taste. This time, I devoured.

I gripped the backs of her knees, holding her legs apart while I used my mouth on her. Her head fell back, her body writhed. Her cries and gasps echoed the pounding of my own blood.

I licked and sucked, breathing in her scent, drinking in the taste of her arousal. My cock stood achingly hard, straining against my pants.

She cried out as she came, her thighs quivering on either side of my head. I pulled up to find her collapsed on the bed, spread out before me. Her eyes had gone dreamy, her arms flung overhead. She looked amazing. Flushed and sated.

When she reached for my cock, I pulled her hand to my chest instead, held it there.

"Not fair," she murmured. "You always get to do stuff."

"It's okay. Just let me hold you." I drew her against me, hooked an arm around her middle. Sensed the moment she drifted off to sleep.

Easing out of bed, I pulled the covers over her, plumped the pillow under her head. Her breathing stayed slow and even, her features peaceful. I used her wallscreen to leave her a message before heading out.

In the elevator, I sighed. Once again, we'd tried to talk and it'd turned into more. Then again, any thing involving Briar turned into more. My partnership with her evolved into friendship. Our fake status into scalding chemistry.

A relationship wasn't in the works for me. The plan was to get my license and focus on my job.

Being with Briar made me lose sight of that.

The following week, I met Hector at the training course I'd

booked. He ate a nutrient bar as he flicked through his screen, closing it when he saw us approaching.

I pointed a thumb at Tristan. "Invited him along." Though I'd half expected him to refuse my invitation, he'd shown up.

"More the merrier." Hector grinned, offered Tristan a nutrient bar.

The three of us moved through the track's warm up. After gauging our reaction times, I bumped the difficulty. The voice game me a warning about the high intensity. I gave it the go ahead.

The track exploded in a nonstop barrage, designed to push us to our limits. Hector took the lead, flashing in and out of existence, whooping whenever he dodged successfully.

Tristan followed. He wasn't fast, but the guy had power. He didn't use the armor, just raw strength, crushing obstacles with his bare hands.

I filled in the blanks, watching both their backs as I kept us moving forward. I'd never run the course on such a high level. It was frantic. Dummies popped out of nowhere. Obstacles rushed us from the sides, plummeted from the ceiling. Explosions and lights assaulted my senses.

By the time we reached the end, the track was a wreckage. Dummies lay ripped in half, innards spilling. Blaster cannons folded in on themselves. Barricades crushed. The three of us were pouring sweat.

The screen scrolled out the numbers. Hector whistled. "Nice!" He held up his hand to Tristan.

I studied the stats while the two of them high-fived. "Little slow on the blinds. But not bad."

We left the training course and hit the gym. After the frantic energy in the course, the gym seemed a haven of calm repetition and studied movement. The smell of rubber and clean, circulating air washed over me.

While Tristan opted for the climbing wall, Hector took the running station next to mine. "So, I was thinking."

"What'd I tell you about limits, Diaz?"

"Your lady friend's got two roommates, right?"

"Forget it."

"Not like that. Game night. Board games, movies. A little down time before the midterm insanity overtakes us."

I adjusted my pace, considered. "Maybe." When Hector gawked at me, I frowned. "What?"

"Wasn't expecting you to agree. You're usually all work and then more work."

I couldn't argue. "I'll ask Briar."

The phrase sounded weird. As if we were a couple, conferring with one another before committing to plans. The reluctance to draw a hard line with her was a warning, clear as day, that I needed a line. Badly.

The uneasy feeling stayed with me, rising to the surface whenever I wasn't in class or training. By the following week, I was no closer to an answer.

I got to Jubilee's early, settled in with an iced green tea and an apple. I lost myself in studying for awhile, going over notes from class, reviewing for midterms. I quick drafted a short paper for my Principles of Emergency Management class, sent an email to my biology professor about one of the readings.

I glanced at the time, frowned. Nearly thirty minutes had passed.

I started to ping Briar when the doors opened. She strode through, her expression tight, brows drawn together.

"Sorry I'm late." She rushed to the table, dumped her bag as she slid into the seat across from mine. "I'm parched. I wonder if they have any of those berry spritzers in stock."

"What's wrong?"

She tensed, then jerked a shoulder. "Family drama. No big deal."

When I took her hand, she exhaled. "Okay, maybe it's a big deal." Her voice trembled.

I tugged her out of the chair. "Come on."

"The report."

"Later."

We gathered our stuff and left the coffeehouse. "Where to?" Briar asked.

"The arboretum."

"I've never been."

"You'll like it." I hoped she would. Anything to take the miserable expression off her face.

Damn. Hadn't I decided I to step back? Though the minute I saw her, heard her voice, the discipline I'd built over the years crumbled. It was frustrating as hell.

And a little terrifying.

26 LULLABY

Even after a year living on campus, the institute's size amazed me. The campus sprawled over most of what used to be the Mayport Naval Base, over 3000 acres. There were entire sections I hadn't visited, areas I didn't even know existed.

This one was beautiful, a lush, green oasis. Vibrant trees spread leaf-filled branches, offering shade from the Florida sun. Tidy gravel paths branched off in roving directions around a small, clear pond ringed by pruned bushes and shrubs. Cultivated flowers speared from beds, colorful blossoms waving in the breeze.

"It's gorgeous," I said, breathing in the fresh scent of cut grass and water. Twigs and gravel crunched underfoot while branches rustled overhead.

Jase kept hold of my hand as he guided me along one of the paths. It brought us to a small, old green house. The walls were paneled glass panes, the white paint faded and flaking. Vines crept over the sides, brought to mind quaint British countryside cottages.

"Into horticulture?" I asked.

"I was hunting for some place quiet." He grabbed the door knob, jiggled.

It held firm.

My shoulders drooped. I'd been looking forward to seeing Jase's secret hideaway.

I was about to recommend we go back to my place when he leaned in to study the glass panels on either side of the door. He ran his hand over the frame, tested the edges. Then he unclipped the utility tool on his belt.

"What are you doing?" I asked, watching as he flicked open one of the knives.

He studied the blade, pushed it down, flicked open a different one. "Getting us in."

I held my breath as he slid the blade under the glass. The faint screech of metal against glass set my teeth on edge. The pane shifted as he gently levered it up and down, side to side.

The glass slid up from the bottom edge. Jase coaxed it forward, his eyes focused. He worked his fingers underneath, slid the pane free from the frame.

A second later, he hooked his arm through the opening, jiggled the handle. The door swung open with a faint creak.

He closed the tool, replaced the glass panel, leaving no signs of a break in.

"How'd you learn to do that?" I asked.

"I'm not as good a guy as you think."

The grim expression on his face when he said it pulled at me. "That's definitely not true." I grabbed his hand, squeezed. "You suck at racing games, but you're great otherwise."

His lips twitched. He gave me a light kiss before leading the way into the greenhouse.

It obviously hadn't been used in awhile. A few discarded potting tools sat atop the bare tables. Empty terra cotta plant

pots and plastic watering cans stacked in the corner, gathering
dust. Dried leaves crunched underfoot, crumbling to dust as I
trod over them.

"Feel better?" Jase asked.

"Did I look bad?"

"Sad. Angry."

Picking up a dried flower petal, I rubbed it between my
fingers. "My uncle's been giving me a hard time. He always
wanted abilities. He's tried all kinds of therapy, medical trials,
experimental stuff. None of it works of course, but he was
desperate."

"When my power manifested, he decided I'm the family's
one shot at superpowered glory. When I was younger, I used to
wish I could give him my ability instead of keeping it for
myself."

"What about now?" Jase asked.

"I'm not sure," I admitted. I liked myself, but I figured I'd
be okay even without powers. My uncle was another story.

I let the petal dust fall from my fingers. "It's even worse
now. He's got it in his head if I'm not outperforming everyone
else, then I must not be trying. And lately he's been sending me
wild news stories. One was about a girl who went missing near
here. I guess he thinks it'll keep me on my toes if I know how
dangerous the world is."

"Sounds tough."

"It is, sometimes. He took us in after my mom left us, paid
for everything I needed. We owe him a lot." I let out a shaky
exhale. "Anyway, it's just until I graduate."

Jase started to speak, stopped. "If you need help." he said at
last. "I'm here."

The offer warmed me. "Thanks for bringing me here. It's
quiet and kind of mysterious. Like we're in a children's mystery
novel."

"Searching for the lost key to the attic?"

"Picking locks seems handy for solving mysteries." When he stared at the ground, I pulled at his hand until he turned toward me.

Silence stretched. I waited, hoping. We'd gone through a field exercise together, slogged through research articles, been intimate.

But Jase was such a guarded person. He held himself a little distant, a little apart. I wanted to know more about him. Not just out of curiosity, but because it'd be a sign he trusted me.

He hesitated, then said, "Both my parents are Aegis."

"So they fight..." I hesitated.

"Villains." He said the word in a flat, cold tone.

Criminal PNs. It happened, of course. We're people. Some used their abilities to hurt others, to steal wealth, to gain power. Aegis task forces worked alongside normie law enforcement to hunt criminal PNs and bring them to justice.

It sounds like real superhero type stuff. However the high mortality rate, coupled with the increased incidents of mental and physical trauma, made being an Aegis agent one of the most dangerous positions for PNs.

"They must be tough," I said.

"They are. I'm the weak one. I used my ability to do stupid shit. I'd jump off roofs, get into fights."

"A rebellious phase." Not uncommon among PNs. Still, hard to imagine it happening to Jase.

"My parents are the epitome of Powerhouses," he continued. "Wanted me to take on the mantel of what it meant to be a PN. Of course, that made me run out and do more stupid shit. I ran with a crew. Most of them were in that life because they didn't have a choice. It was the only way for them to survive."

His stared at the ground, voice quieting. "I was there because it pissed off my parents. Fault, huh?"

"I'm not here to judge you." I kept my voice gentle. "I'm here to listen."

He paused, flexed his hands. "Being Aegis, my parents travel a lot. Cassi basically raised me. Even though I made her life hell. I owe it to her to do things right this time."

I bit my lip. He was finally opening up. On the other hand, he wasn't telling me everything.

Deciding to leave things for the time being, I wrapped my arms around his middle. "Thank you for sharing a piece of yourself with me."

He gripped my waist, lifted and set me on the edge of one of the tables. He stood between my parted knees, hands braced on the table on either side of my thighs.

He lowered his head, bringing his strong features close to mine. This close, I could see my reflection in his near-black eyes.

"I don't know how much I have to give, Briar." The words came out rough, tight.

The emotion in his voice made my chest clutch. I wrapped my legs around his middle, pulling him closer. Cupping his jaw in my palm, I pressed a kiss to one side of his mouth, then to the other, then right on his lips. "You have plenty to give." Grinning, I squeezed his biceps. "See?"

He chuckled, a low rumble of sound. "You just want me for my body."

"It is a nice one." I indulged myself by running my palms over his sculpted pecs. "Beyond that, we're project partners, fellow Powerhouses. And, I hope, friends." I wanted to add "maybe more," but I held back.

The tightness in his expression eased. "Friends."

"Although the body part is pretty good."

He laughed. Straightening, he cupped my ass, squeezed. "Yeah, it is."

Thrilled at the bold contact, I pressed my breasts against him. "In fact, further study is needed."

"Another project." His mouth brushed over mine. "Better get to it."

The kiss went from slow and sweet to scorching. A wet tangle of tongues and lips. He pulled my ass forward until I was almost off the table, held up only by his big hands. The position spread my legs wide, letting him nestle against me. Even through our clothes, I felt the hard press of his erection.

I shivered, struggling to grind against him. Frustrated, I scratched my nails over the back of his neck, nipped at his lips.

Jase groaned, ground against me hard. "I'm this close to shoving into you, here and now."

The idea thrilled me. Sex, with Jase, outside where anyone might see us.

"But?" I asked, sensing it coming.

"I don't know if I'm ready." He cupped my jaw. "You're not just a fuck partner or a project partner or a friend."

My heart clutched. He was telling me I was special to him.

I covered his hands with mine, basking in his touch. "You're important to me, too. No need to rush." I paused. "Well, maybe a small need."

He skimmed a thumb over my breast. "Just a small one?"

I arched, both nipples turning to hard peaks. "Okay, a big roaring one. But I want us both to want it."

"I do want you, Briar. Badly." He rested his brow against mine. "Give me a little more time."

"Sure. And next time, I get to do stuff."

"Making demands?"

"You bet."

As we left the arboretum, I thought over what he'd told me.

Wondered what'd happened to put him off relationships. He'd mentioned ruining Cassi's life. Alba said they'd been through enough.

I held back the questions roiling inside of me. The more I learned about Jase, the less I seemed to understand.

27 STRONGHOLD

Hector grinned as the three of us piled into the elevator. "This place is beyond. Think they'd let me jump off the roof into the pool?"

I adjusted my cuff buttons. "Definitely not."

"I'm keyed. Midterms are over and I'm not failing anything."

"Yet."

Tristan stood behind us, saying nothing.

The three of us were dressed for the evening. I'd gone with dark grey. Hector wore a black vest over a blood red shirt. Tristan, no surprise, full black.

The elevator doors pinged open. "Hi!" One of Briar's roommates, a slim brunette, poked her head around the corner. "Come on in."

Beside me, Hector froze. "Hazel."

"Hector?" Her dress shimmered blue-green as she threw her arms around him. "It's been awhile."

Hector tensed, didn't hug her back. "Yeah, it has."

"Hi, I'm Hazel," she said to me.

"Jase. This is Tristan."

"Make yourselves at home." She led the way, calling out to the others.

"Alright?" I asked Hector as we settled into the living room.

"What? Oh, yeah. Fine." He shook his head, like a man waking up.

Briar stepped out of her room, smiling as she came towards me. She was wearing a short dress the color of ripe peaches and gold heels with straps wrapped up her calves to her knees.

Her other roommate, Lucie, poured everyone cocktails. While the group mixed, I took Briar's hand. "Nice dress."

Her brows lifted. "The first time, you didn't say much."

"I was trying to control myself. You looked good enough to eat."

"And tonight?"

"You know the first thought I had about you?"

"That I was a jerk for leaving you in an elevator?"

I moved closer to speak into her ear. "That you're a stunner, Briar. I think it every time I see you."

She blushed, her shoulders lifting towards her ears. "All this praise is embarrassing."

I pulled her in for a quick kiss. "Get used to it."

We talked, polished off the cocktails, then piled into the BlackbirdPre I'd hired for the evening. It reached downtown, and the six of us climbed out of the car, crowding onto the curb. The mid-October air was cool and humid, the sky overhead a faded black against the bright city lights.

The line in front of the club stretched around the block. Extra security personnel, privately hired PNs in sharp black suits, stood along the walkway. Low tempo music piped through the outdoor speakers, just audible over the sounds of traffic and voices.

Briar's hand brushed against my arm. "Ready?"

Her eyes widened as I slid an arm around her waist. I hooked my hand around her hip, tucked her close to my side. "Now I am."

Cassi met as personally at the door, smiling even as she rushed us through the entrance. Cool air washed over me from the vents. Music crashed down on us, the lights flaring and pulsing over the crowd.

"It's insane tonight!" she yelled over the pounding rhythm and answering screams in the crowd. "Here." She passed out sheets of holotatts.

I slapped mine on my wrist. The thin sheet adhered to my skin. It activated at once, the image of an Iceberg glowing faintly, with the letters VIP scripted underneath. It shifted colors now and then, from gleaming white to pale blue to striking purple.

"You guys can use them at the bar, too." She grinned. "On Jase, of course."

"Thanks," Briar said, the others echoing her.

"Enjoy yourselves." Cassi slanted a quick look at me, tipped her head to one side.

"I'll be right back," I said, leaning over to kiss Briar. Her lashes fluttered closed, her chin tipped up. Her pale pink lips parted as she waited.

Seeing her vulnerable, expectant, twisted me in knots. I wanted to yank her against me, kiss her until we both forgot everything except each other.

I brushed my lips over hers. "Stay out of trouble."

While the others headed to the bar, I followed Cassi up the stairs to the office. The metal rungs clanged underfoot as we climbed to the second floor. The crash of music and crowd faded from a roar to dull thumping as I shut the door behind us.

Cassi wandered over to the mini fridge, dug out a can of

Rocket water. "So, what's the what?" she asked, pouring it into two glasses.

I tensed. "You only use that phrase when you're about to drop a bomb on me."

She scowled, tossed in lime slices and tiny straws. "It's annoying how well you know me."

I took the drink she handed me. Held it while I waited.

"Okay, okay." She set her drink aside, clasped her hands. "I don't know how to say this."

I frowned. "Whatever it is, we'll deal—"

"I'm going to ask Alba to marry me." When I stared at her, she burst into laughter. "Oh my God, I said it!"

My mind blanked out. One second, I'd been imagining dire scenarios. Now I was getting a sister-in-law.

I recovered. "Great. It's great."

"Really?"

"You kidding? It's fucking fantastic." I set the drink down, gathered her in for a big hug. "Congratulations."

She laughed. "I'm thrilled. And terrified!"

My stomach tightened at the joy on my sister's face. God knew she deserved it.

"You're a good brother. It's true. I wasn't always there for you, plus I set you up on some, uh, not great dates."

"You wanted me to be happy."

"I did. I do. I know you blame yourself for what happened. You've got to let go and live your life."

"My life's good as it is."

"You make plans for what you have to do, not what you want to do." She grabbed my hands, stared at me in earnest. "Decide what it is you want and go for it. Nothing would make me happier."

I thought about my sister's words as I took the stairs. For so long I'd been working to to pay her back, to undo the wrongs I'd committed. Thinking somehow, it'd make up for everything that'd happened.

I paused, one hand on the rail. The choices I'd made in life, from education to career to personal, I'd done it with that end in mind. I went to class, I trained, I studied. I was disciplined but I took no joy or pride in it. Just another step on the ladder.

Towards what? Was there anything I'd chosen because I'd wanted it?

The pulsing sounds of the crowd reached a crescendo. I reached the ground floor just as the lights flashed and shifted. They slid over the crowd and, for a moment, illuminated Briar. She danced, arms held high, hair flying. She paused to listen and laugh at something Hector said.

Her gaze shifted, met mine, and she smiled.

My chest tightened and I swallowed hard. Briar was the hitch in my plans. The one thing I hadn't counted on. The one thing I wanted for myself.

Easy to tell, because I worked hard to deny it.

I strode across the dance floor, the crowd easing around me as I made my way to her. My hands went to her waist, molding her to me. The soft rounds of her breasts pushed against me. I caught her scent, the sweet fragrance of vanilla. It made me want to bury my face in her hair and breath deep.

Instead, I gave her a hard kiss. She tensed for a moment before responding, her palms sliding over my chest. Her head tilted, her lips parting to give me full access to her mouth.

I took, demanded. Kissed her until she moaned. I drank in the sound, the hum of her voice. It filled me until I ached.

It wasn't nearly enough.

A whoop rent the air behind us. "Floor show!" Hector yelled.

Hazel rolled her eyes, elbowed him.

Briar gave me a questioning look. Her cheeks were flushed,

her lips kiss-swollen. As much as I wanted to carry her off somewhere private, I knew she'd want to see the show.

I spun her around, pressing her back against me so she faced the floating stage. Lowering my head, I gave her a nip on the ear. "Tonight. After the show. You're all mine."

T he night was starting out promising.

The dance floor was elbow to elbow, a huge undulating wave of people. I let myself move and drift to the music, the throbbing pulse echoing through my body.

Lucie spun and swayed, graceful even in sky high heels. Hector was speaking to Hazel, making her laugh. Tristan sat at the bar observing the scene, his drink held loosely in one hand. I had yet to hear the guy speak, but he didn't seem uncomfortable.

Hands gripped me. Before I could speak, Jase had pulled me in and kissed me senseless.

"Tonight. After the show. You're all mine."

Jase's voice rumbled through me, leaving my skin humming. The music swayed and I moved with it, leaning back against him.

He growled, grip tightening on my waist, fingers pressing into my skin. "Watch it, or I won't be able to wait."

I started to reply when the music shifted. The lights changed, flashing from deep purple to an icy blue. The hover platform rose, disappearing into the ceiling before lowering once again, this time with a different set. A hologram shimmered around the platform and settled into place, an enormous glacier on a frozen ocean. Waves of cold fog rolled off it, sending chills cascading over my skin.

The glacier burst, pouring shimmers of light into the air. AlterEgo stood on the platform, wearing pristine white suits.

The crowd screamed as the band hefted their electric string instruments, each clear as glass. Nolan Lane, lead violinist and sexy musical genius, gave us a searing look as the first notes crashed through the air.

The dance floor roared. The other members joined in, the soaring voices of the strings twining with the throbbing electronic background beats.

I whooped and danced along with the others, let myself get carried by the atmosphere. The music thrumming my senses, the thud of my feet against the dance floor. The song ended, the club a riot of sound and color.

Through it, I felt Jase's presence. Watching me, waiting.

My blood pounded as I whirled around, linked my arms around his neck. "Now."

His hands streaked up my back, molding to my curves. "You're sure?" His voice came out low and rough.

"Beyond."

Turning, he met Hector's gaze. Hector smirked and gave us a thumbs up.

I stopped long enough to speak to Hazel and Lucie. They both waved me off as I hurried to the door. Jase waited for me, his body tense. He grabbed my hand and we hurried from the club and into Jase's car.

We tumbled into the backseat. The door barely slid shut when he was on me, hands roaming my body, his mouth hot on mine. I laid on my back, my legs hooking around his hips. He settled his weight between my thighs, his erection grinding against me.

"I'm implanted," I said as he fondled my breast through my dress. My nipples hardened to stiff peaks, straining against the fabric.

"Me, too." He ducked his head to bite and kiss my neck. "Fuck, you're driving me crazy."

My sex clenched, my wetness soaking my panties. I arched against him, thrilled when he ground against me. I reached for his fly.

A soft voice chimed, "Sexual activity is not advised while the vehicle is in motion."

Jase glowered at the controls. "Cockblocked by my own car."

"We'll be there soon."

"Not soon enough." He sat up, dragging me along to straddle his lap. His warm, wide palm smoothed over the bare skin of my thigh, toyed with the edge of my panties.

"Ace is watching," I said, angling my head to kiss him.

"Let him." His teeth scraped my bottom lip, sending chills dancing down my back. I responded by scratching my fingernails over the back of his neck, reveling in the rough touch of his hands on my bare legs.

By the time the ride ended, we were both taught and aching, sprinting from the car to the front door. In the elevator, I flung myself at him, crushing my breasts against his chest. He lifted me, holding me against him, hooking my legs around his waist.

The doors opened, the apartment lights flaring to life. Jase's cupped my ass, holding me steady as he marched across the apartment in a fast, determined clip.

He tossed me on the bed, making me laugh. He stepped

back, staring at me as I lay sprawled on top of the blankets. "I've been wanting this. Wanting you."

Thrilled, and not willing to wait a second longer, I rose to my knees. Grabbed the bottom of his shirt and undid the buttons. I bit my lip at the sight of his long, lean torso. The flex and stretch of muscles beneath his golden skin. The soft, dark trail of fine hair that disappeared beneath the band of his pants.

He dropped to his knees. Our lips met while he tugged the zipper of my dress, eased the garment off my body. He untied my heels, unhooked my bra, spilling my breasts.

Our kissing grew more rushed, frantic. I wriggled free from my clothes, my eyes devouring him as he shoved out of his pants. His erection jutted, hard and hot and heavy.

He knelt in front of me again, cupped my breasts. He took first one nipple, then the other into his mouth. I arched into the sensation, feeling it echo between my legs. I tangled my fingers in his hair, tugged hard.

He shifted forward and I fell onto my back, my legs parting as he braced himself over me. His fingers sought my clit, teased it until I writhed against the sheets.

"Briar." His tip nudged at my entrance, firm and smooth.

"Yes, now." I gasped as he slid inside me. He didn't stop, plunging into me with one long, smooth thrust until he was buried deep. I cried out at the sudden possession, the shock of our bodies joining.

He braced his hands on either side of my head. The muscles in his arms and shoulders bulged as he began to thrust. Each time he did, he sank into me deep. My sex stretched around him, aching with exquisite fullness. Every part of my body sang in triumph. I'd wanted this, him, for so long. Now he was over me, inside me.

Mine.

He set a firm, fast rhythm, demanding I keep up. I grasped

at the covers, felt the erotic bounce of my breasts with each thrust. My muscles tensed, my back arched as I climbed higher, straining for that peak.

He gripped the back of my knee, pushing it towards my shoulder to spread me wider. "Come hard," he demanded. His other hand slid between us, his thumb circling my clit even as he maintained his relentless pace.

The climax welled within me, a crashing tide. I screamed as it broke over me, rocking me to my core. My body spasmed, shuddering and clenching around him.

"Again. More." He thrust into me hard and fast. One of his hands plucked at my nipples, brought them to stiff points before sliding down to massage my clit again. The sound of our strained voices and the slapping of our bodies filled the air.

I came again, shuddering, thighs shaking. Jase's mouth covered mine, drank in my gasps until, breathing hard, he braced himself on straight arms to pump into my body.

I watched, fascinated, as he came. The muscles of his shoulders and arms bunched, his eyes closing, his brows drawing together as he gave a low, strained groan.

He sank on top of me, his warm, heavy weight pressing me to the bed. I sighed as he eased out of me, relishing in the delicious ache that followed.

Jase's fingers went to my sex, caressing my slick folds. "You're soaked," he said, giving me a smile that was pure, satisfied male.

"Who's fault is that?" My voice came out raspy.

"Yours. For being so sexy."

"It's the burden I bear. You're the one who has to suffer."

"Someone's got to." He lay on his side, his head propped on his elbow. With his mussed hair, the feral gleam in his eyes, he was like a warrior in repose. His mouth curved in a lazy, smug smile. Flashed me that elusive dimple.

I snuggled against him, seeking his warmth. He tugged the blanket over my bare legs, tucked it around me.

My heart knocked against my ribs. When I'd first met Jase, I'd thought we were too different to be together. He was too elite, too far out of my reach. I'd fluffed my comfort zone into a nest I never wanted to leave.

But lying with him felt close. Intimate.

I was pondering this when his fingers slipped into me. I tipped my head back when he sought my throat with his teeth.

"Not finished yet," he growled, fingers sliding out to tease my clit.

I made a pleased sound, gripped his wrist to stop him. "I want to do stuff this time."

He chuckled, leaned back against the pillows. Offering me the full view of his amazing body. "Do as you please."

I did.

29 STRONGHOLD

"That concludes the lesson on early emotional attachment. Be sure to do the extra readings before next week."

Dr. Singh turned from the wallscreen as it powered off and the lights came on. "Also, your midterm exam scores and the scores from the most recent field exercises will be posted over the next few days."

She nodded when the class groaned. "My condolences. I'll see you next week. Jase, a moment?"

The window covers slid towards the ceiling, pouring light into the room. The rest of the class filed out the doors or, in the case of one woman, walked straight through the wall. Expressions ranged from exhausted to zoned out to grim determination. Typical among the student population.

The sound of footsteps and voices receded as I grabbed my bag, headed for the podium.

"It's about your most recent scores," Dr. Singh said once we were alone.

I gripped my bag strap. "Bad?"

"Comparatively, they're high. For you, they're not what I'd

normally expect. Your midterms were inconsistent with your previous performance. For the field exercise, you were late noticing the withdraw signal."

The latter stung. Exams were one thing. They only effected me. My field performance effected my team.

"I didn't pull you aside to berate you. You're one of our best performing students across the board." She settled into the edge of the desk. "I wanted to ask if everything's okay."

I raked a hand through my hair. "There's a lot going on right now."

"Perhaps you'd consider scaling back."

I leaned back. "You mean drop a class?"

"Or cut volunteer hours or pass on the squad leader position. Classes, work, the project. Cutting yourself slack allows you to put yourself whole-heartedly into what's left." When I said nothing, she sighed. "Think about it and come talk to me."

I mulled over the professor's words on the drive back to my apartment. The idea of letting something, anything, go made my gut twist. Maybe for others, cutting back was an option.

To me, it sounded like I couldn't keep up. Like I wasn't good enough.

What the hell would I even cut? I needed all my classes to maintain honors level. Volunteer work was out of the question. The reason I was doing this was to help people. I had to stay a squad leader. It was the best way to gain field experience and get noticed by recruiters.

What was left? I flicked open my schedule. Block to block classes, appointments, study sessions. Every hour, every minute, accounted for.

I found a tiny sliver, color coded sky blue. "Dinner + Project. Briar's. Bring dessert."

I smiled. It'd been three weeks since Briar and I had gone

from fake to real. Three weeks of being together both as
partners and as lovers.

"I want to do things right this time," I'd said the night after
we'd finished our second round of mind-blowing sex.

She'd curled up with her back to me, our bodies spooned
together. Her ass nestled to my front, my knees tucked against
the backs of hers.

She traced her fingertip around on my palm, making little
patterns. "I should've told you a long time ago how I felt."

"Me first." I turned her in my arms, held her against me. "I
want to date you. For real this time."

"Me, too."

Hearing the catch in her voice, I rubbed her back.
"Alright?"

She burrowed in, her face against my chest. "Just happy."

I hoped that was all. I didn't want Briar to think she needed
to hold back on anything. Though that wasn't fair.

I still hadn't told her everything.

Since then, we'd settled into an equilibrium. With just over
a month until final exams, most of our dates were spent
working on the project or having study sessions over dinner.

I exhaled, leaned back in the seat. I appreciated Dr. Singh's
concern, but scaling back was out of the question.

My HC pinged. I tapped it open.

PARKCASSILTD: Heeeey! Still on for lunch?
    STRONGHOLD: Sure.
PARKCASSILTD: Invite Briar!! :)

Not a bad idea. If I invited her over, the three of us could eat
together. Then once Cassi left, I'd coax Briar into bed.

I sent her a message and, remembering her sweet tooth, put in a delivery order for cookies. Chocolate chip.

By the time I arrived at my apartment, the cookies had been delivered by a bot. The container sat on the kitchen counter along with a note from the store thanking me for my patronage.

I set down my bag, paused at the sound of someone in the apartment. "Hey, sis. You got here fast."

A husky, feminine voice responded. "Domesticity doesn't suit you."

That voice. Every cell in my body went on defense, my ability lighting up.

Jaw tight, I marched into the living area.

A young woman stood near the windows, leaning against one wall. Mink brown hair cascaded around a long, pretty face with light skin and big brown eyes. She was eating one of the cookies.

My fists clenched. "Landmine. What the fuck are you doing here?"

"Parole." She winked, nibbled at the cookie. "I'm a good girl, you know. A cinch to get in here. Don't forget, I taught you everything you know about breaking in."

"Get the hell out."

"Is this any way to welcome an old friend, Jase? Or, rather, Overwhelm?"

The name made my blood boil. Made me remember a dumbass kid who thought himself invincible.

She finished the cookie, licked her thumb. "Aren't you curious about why I'm here?"

"Not interested." My muscles bunched, ready to drag her out on her ass.

She tilted her head. "Are you really going to start a fight here? There are families on this floor. One right below. It'd be a shame if bystanders got caught up. Then your sister will have to bail you out for violence. Again."

Cassi's face flashed in my mind. Her hands shaking whenever she signed release forms, made excuses for me.

I ground my teeth hard enough to send bolts of pain through my head. "What do you want?"

"I'm here to extend an invitation. I'm putting together a new crew and I need muscle. Which I happen to know you have in abundance."

"Not interested in joining a bunch of lowlives."

"I've outgrown petty crimes. And, well, let's say we've got a seal of approval. It's practically legit."

"You come in here telling me this and I'm supposed to let you leave?"

"Oh, you'll let me. After all, I haven't done anything. We talked. Reminisced. Like old friends."

"Get out. Now."

"If you change your mind, ping me on Impulse." She made for the door, paused near me. Close enough I caught a whiff of her jasmine perfume. "You can pretend for everyone else. I know the real you, Overwhelm."

30 STRONGHOLD

T he door clicked shut behind her.

I raked my hands through my hair, tried to get a grip on the rage inside me. It writhed inside of me, a black beast of fury, clawing to get free. If I unleashed it, there'd be no coming back.

I threw the cookies into the recomposter. I didn't want to eat anything Landmine had touched.

Thinking of Briar, I sent her a message.

STRONGHOLD: Raincheck.

A video call notification pinged. I rubbed the back of my neck, accepted.

Briar appeared on the screen, her brows lifted. "You okay?"

"Fine."

She frowned. "Are you in trouble? Let me help."

"Leave it, Briar." My voice came out curt, clipped.

Her expression tightened. The call ended.

I scrubbed a hand over my face, exhaled. The doorscreen chimed, alerting me that Cassi had arrived in the building. I fought to gather myself while I waited.

"Hey, I'm here." She breezed in, set the bags on the wraparound bar. "Where's Briar?"

I hesitated. Part of me wanted to tell her about Landmine's visit. But she'd been happy lately. Focused on the club, on Alba.

I wasn't going to wreck her life. Not again.

The thought she might've been here when Landmine arrived made my blood run cold. I needed to keep her, them, out of this. For her sake.

"Raincheck," I said, opening the takeout boxes. Korean food. Steamed rice, bulgogi, bright red kimchi.

We settled on stools, spread the food out on the bar. The taste slammed me into the past. Mornings fighting with Cassi, nights spent sneaking out to steal and fight. My parents' exasperation when I got another notice from school.

"You're more broody than usual." Cassi dug into the food. "What's wrong?"

"Midterm results." The half-lie left a bitter taste in my mouth.

"Don't push yourself too much. It's okay to take things slow. No rush to live your life. I'll ask Briar to keep you out of trouble."

I grimaced. "Yeah."

She narrowed her eyes. "What did you do?"

"Why's it my fault?"

"Because you're a lummox. Did you say something stupid? Go and apologize."

"I didn't. Well, I did." Fuck, my thoughts were mixed up.

"You've been dating forever, I'm sure you can figure out a way to apologize."

"It's only been a few weeks." Realizing my slip, I froze.

"No, it's been months. Since the beginning of the semester." When I hesitated, she frowned. "Jase. What aren't you telling me?"

Lies and excuses swarmed my mind. None of them adequate.

The food sat heavy in my stomach. I put it aside. I was tired of hanging onto this secret. What had it gotten me in the end? I'd hurt Briar and lied to my family.

Time to come clean.

"We weren't together," I said at last.

"What?"

"We weren't romantically involved. Not then, at least. We were faking it."

My sister stiffened. "You lied to me. You and Briar both lied to me."

"It's not Briar's fault. I convinced her to go along with it."

"For God's sake, why?"

"Because I didn't want you to worry about me." It sounded ridiculous when I said it. "You kept shoving these dates my way. I wanted you to focus on your own life."

Cassi shot to her feet. "You are my life! Why don't you get it?"

I stood, glaring. My pulse hammered, building to a crescendo drowning out everything else. "You think I need my sister to set me up? I'm so pathetic I need a pity date?"

"You're pretty pathetic right now," she snapped.

"I did it to get you off my back!" I roared.

Silence filled the air. The blood pounding in my skull receded, my anger cooling and leaving behind a greasy pool of guilt.

Cassi's mouth pressed in a hard line. She stepped back from me. "You're right. I should mind my own business."

My chest tightened. "Sis."

She crossed her arms. "Let's take a break. We'll talk later, okay?"

I swallowed the explanations burning in my throat. "Okay." She was right. Best to take a timeout, come back with a cooler head.

"Whatever's going on between you and Briar, your feelings for her are real. That much I can tell."

The door clicked shut behind her. I sank back on the stool, buried my face in my hands. We'd argued before, but taking out my frustrations on her was inexcusable. All Cassi ever asked of me was I take care of myself. She didn't deserve to be on the receiving end of my bullshit.

Neither did Briar. The memory of her expression made my gut churn. I needed to talk to her. Apologize.

Then again, maybe it was better this way. Putting distance between me and Briar would give me the space to take care of classes, being squad leader.

And Landmine. There were plenty of scumbags she could find for her crew. Did she need me in particular? Or had it been a lie to get under my skin.

Theft had been her crime of choice. Screens, HCs, cars, jewelry. As new and flashy as possible. If stealing was her passion, getting into fights had been her hobby. Rival thieving gangs, her own crew, random strangers. It was how she'd recruited me in the first place.

My pulse thundered in my skull, my lungs tight. My vision faded to red, my muscles bunching. I wanted to pound my fist into something, someone. Wanted to—

A trilling alarm blared. The wallscreen lit with an automated message.

. . .

Severe damage to onsite property detected.
Do you require emergency assistance?

I looked down, my blood running cold.

I'd smashed my fist right through the kitchen counter. It'd caved in, chunks of marble and wood lying in ruins. Dust billowed in the air as food and drink spilled.

I stared at my hand. I hadn't even realized what I'd been doing.

Shaken, I opened my HC, sent a message to maintenance to repair the damage. Activated the cleaning bot.

While it worked, I stared at the place where Landmine had been standing. Both she and my sister claimed to know me. Who was right?

And why the hell didn't I know?

31 LULLABY

I raced alongside the gurney as it hurtled towards emergency surgery. My boots slapped against the linoleum, my ponytail flying out behind me. Doctors and nurses kept pace, speaking fast in clipped medical language.

I kept tight hold of the patient's hand, willing him to live. I slipped a stream of my own energy alongside his, coaxing his into a stronger, steadier current. Even with my assistance, he barely hung on, his body and will exhausted. Blood clung to his skin, its metallic scent mixing with antiseptic and sweat.

I broke contact when we reached the surgery doors, fought to steady my breathing. My pulse hammered, sweat coated my palms. The man was one of several victims from a building collapse. Ambulances screamed as they pulled to the curb outside. Gurneys streamed in, flanked by rushed emergency crews.

I did my best, bolstering as many as possible so they'd make it to surgery on time. Hours passed in a blur of sound and noise.

"That's the last of the criticals," said one of the staff. "Why don't you take a break? Recharge."

I managed a tired smile. "Thanks, I will." Leaving behind the sounds and sights of the emergency wing, I headed to the cafeteria floor.

Cafeteria food is never award winning, but the stuff at Mayport General was decent. The trick was to stay away from anything with gravy or cheese.

I grabbed a plastic tray, weighed my options as I paced the various stations. Free hospital food was one of the perks of my assignment. If crumbly meatloaf and reheated peas could be considered a perk.

Plus I was starving. I'd tapped my entire well bolstering those critical patients. My limbs were leaden, my hands shaky and clammy. My lids drooped with exhaustion. I needed to close the current, not tap into my ability for awhile.

Hopefully a few helpings of sliced peaches would perk me back up.

The dining area sprawled around me as I took a seat near the windows, a gleaming expanse of clean tiles and spotless metal. Patients and staff clustered at tables or near the food stations, picking through bowls of fresh fruit. A smaller buffet offered bottomless coffee and tea. Quiet muzak hummed through the wall speakers, a lulling backdrop to the sounds of shoes against tile and dishes clinking on trays. The air smelled of baked potatoes, coffee, and the faint scent of lemon cleaner.

I glanced at my HC. An email from the institute, a missed call from my uncle, a notification from my Impulse feed.

Seeing Jase's name, I opened the message.

STRONGHOLD: Marked up article attached.

.   .   .

I slumped in my seat. It'd been over a week since he'd canceled on our coffee date. I'd waited for him to call me, tell me what was going on.

Instead, he asked if we could suspend our meetups for awhile. We'd worked on our portions of the project separately, communicating only through messages.

Now it was fall break, and instead of spending it with my boyfriend, I was pulling extra shifts. I'd thought about going home, but I didn't want to deal with my uncle, so I'd made excuses about work.

I stirred granola into my cup of chocolate-strawberry yogurt. Was Jase having second thoughts about us? If that was the case, why not tell me? He didn't seem like the kind of guy to leave his girlfriend hanging.

That uneasy feeling I sometimes got around him returned. Did I know Jase or didn't I? I wanted to poke and pry, but worried that would make him withdraw further.

Someone approached my table, paused near my elbow. "Briar, right?"

I looked up to find a familiar young woman. She carried a tray piled high with chip bags.

"Serena. From sociology and Jase's squad."

"Oh, sure. Sit. Are you sick?"

"Visiting a family member." She slid into the seat across from me. "Work detail, huh? And then you have to deal with Jase."

She laughed, opened a bag of pizza flavored chips. "Don't get up in arms. I mean the guy's temperamental. Mr. Efficient one moment, hot-headed the next. He's a good leader, but he drops balls. The last field exercise? Bombed."

I frowned. The idea of Jase bombing anything seemed impossible.

She crunched through the bag, opened a second one of

honey barbecue. "He's got latent family members, right? I'm writing a paper for Linden's class. Jase promised to answer my questionnaire. Now I'm left hanging."

"My uncle's a latent, and I know Jase's sister. I can help."

"Seriously? Beyond. I'll send you the questionnaire." We exchanged contact info. "My kid sister's latent, too. She cried about it growing up, wondering why she was the only one in our family."

I thought about my uncle's stern expression, the bitterness in his eyes. "I get it."

"It's why I'm taking Linden's class. It'd be beyond if something came out of it."

It was true. Linden's research might have major implications for why certain people manifested powers and others didn't. If there was even a small possibility of helping my uncle, I wouldn't hesitate.

Serena passed me a snack bag. "Didn't mean to talk bad about your boyfriend, ignore me if you want. Jase is the epitome of a Powerhouse. However once he gets tunnel vision, everything else falls to the wayside. Including his friends."

After she left, I stared at the jalapeño flavored chips, my thoughts tumbling together in a big mess.

Serena called Jase hot-headed. A few months ago, I would've dismissed the label outright.

Now, I wasn't certain. I remembered his expression the last time we'd spoken. Instead of calm and controlled, he'd been furious.

I rubbed my arms. Jase wasn't the kind of guy I imagined myself falling for. He didn't listen to music or binge watch tv. He had a gym schedule and absurdly high ambitions.

In spite of that, I wanted to be with him. Wanted the touch of his hands, the flash of his dimple, the strong presence he brought to my life.

If he didn't want me in his, then I needed to know.

I dumped my tray, changed back into plain clothes. I spent the skyrail ride answering Serena's questionnaire. Basic stuff about work, day to day life. While I filled it in, I ate half the bag of chips. A girl needed fuel when confronting her stubborn, surly boyfriend.

It was mid-afternoon by the time I arrived at his building. I steeled my spine and marched to the intercom, pressed the button for Jase's floor.

No answer.

I jabbed it over and over, ignoring the automated voice warning me security would be summoned if I continued.

The screen finally flashed to life. When he saw me, Jase's scowl shifted to a closed expression. "Briar."

"We need to talk. Don't you dare give me the 'now's not a good time' line."

"Now's not a good time."

I crossed my arms. Inside, my stomach twisted into knots. I forced myself to speak rather than slink away in defeat. "Fine. Guess I'll just keep mashing this button until I get arrested." I proceeded to mash.

Swearing, Jase closed the screen. The doors and elevator activated a second later.

I climbed in, tapping my foot as it carried me to Jase's floor. The doors opened and I squared my shoulders as I entered the apartment.

Jase stood in front of the windows, his outline dark against the skyline. He kept his back to me as he spoke. "What do you want?"

32 STRONGHOLD

"I wanted to make sure you're alive." Briar crossed the room, dropping her bag on the bed.

"I'm fine."

"Don't lie to me. Don't push me out of your life."

Pressure built in my chest, squeezed my throat. "You're going to save me? Change me?"

"You think that's what I'm trying to do?"

I crossed my arms. "Wouldn't be the first time someone thought they could." It drew some people, the knowledge that I had a past riddled with violence and danger. Some sought to reform me. Others just wanted to fuck me.

"I'm not 'someone.' We're partners. Friends." Her breath caught. "If you don't want me anymore, then say it."

"It's not you. Dammit." I raked my hands through my hair. "That sounds fucking pathetic."

I stiffened when she reached out, cupped my face in her palms.

"Tell me what's going on," she said.

I swallowed, the gentleness of her touch shaking me.

"Remember I told you I used to run with a bad crowd? One of them contacted me the other day."

"What did they want?"

"Wants me to rejoin the gang." I snorted. "We called ourselves a gang, but we were just a bunch of punks."

"Then they're going to have to look elsewhere. You obviously don't want to go back."

"I couldn't forgive myself if you got hurt over this."

Her hands circled my waist to link at my back. "Thank you for wanting to protect me. I can take care of myself."

"Not by yourself."

"Then we take care of each other. Your way's too one sided." She tilted her head. "Or do you think I'm a wimp?"

"You're not." I gave in to the urge to put my arms around her. "Not even a little bit."

"Maybe a little. Scary movies get to me."

I cupped the back of her head, my fingers sinking into her soft gold hair. "Kind of the point."

"Why are they focused on you? Surely they could get other members way more easily." When I hesitated, she poked me in the chest. "You're still not telling me something. Don't you dare pull the 'for your safety' line."

I closed my eyes. If I told her, I might lose her. It shook me how much I wanted to keep her. In my arms, in my life.

Briar pulled me over to the bed, nudged me until I sat. Sitting beside me, she waited.

"I'm the reason they went to jail." Memories crashed into me as I spoke. For the first time in my life, I didn't shove them into the darkest corners of my head.

Instead, I let them come.

The only sounds other than the constant wail of far off police cars was the rhythmic thud of my fist. At fourteen, I was lanky, hands and feet too big for my body. But I knew how to use them, where to land a blow so it did the most damage.

A hand on my shoulder. Landmine's sultry smile. "Enough, Overwhelm. He can't talk if he's dead."

I spat. I wasn't ready to stop. As long as I was fighting, drinking, stealing, fucking, I wasn't feeling.

I stepped back, joined the other members of our growing crew. Around us lay the collapsed bodies of the rival crew we'd ambushed. They were tough, with a good scattering of PNs, though between me and the twins, our group had the edge.

Ultra grabbed the guy I'd been pounding on, hauled him to his feet. The guy groaned, head lolling. Blood gushed from his nose.

"We wasted a lot of time here with you," asked Landmine. "Make it worth our while. Where you guys headed?"

The guy struggled. When Landmine slapped him, he went limp. "Place off Fifth. We were going to hit it tonight. Soft target. Refurbished electronics. Busted cameras."

Landmine nodded to Ultra, who dropped the guy to the ground.

Landmine and I led the way. I spat again, this time it came out bloody. "We're going to steal a pick?"

"Scared?"

On the contrary, I was hoping more of the other crew would be there already. A solid round with a few more of their members would put me in a good mood.

My pulse hammered in anticipation. My well of power was running low.

Good. A fight was even better when I got bloody.

Landmine purred, stroking her fingers over my arm. "You were made for this life, Overwhelm."

We rounded onto Fifth, studied the small shop's exterior. It sat quiet and dark in a string of other stores, pale orange streetlights throwing shadows against the walls.

Zeal pointed. "Busted security cameras."

We followed the outside of the building until we found a window low enough to bust. I vaulted over the ledge, landed with a thud in the dark interior. The place was quiet as a tomb, the air thick with the smell of dust and brick.

Landmine whooped, eyes bright. "Jackpot, boys. Pick it clean."

The others scattered, shoving HCs and whatever else they could fit into pockets, jackets, down the front of shirts. I skulked around the edges, searching for signs of movement. I didn't need the loot. I wanted action.

A footstep. I spun, eager. I stalked over to where I'd heard the sound, shoved aside a box to find a crouched figure. A man cried out as he fell. I raised my fist, snarling.

Light from the outside slanted across his face. Wrinkles, a trembling chin covered in a cloud of white whiskers.

"No!" he said, bony hands shaking as he lifted them in defense. I waited for him to unleash an ability on me.

Nothing.

I recoiled, my lungs heaving as I stared. He was small. Old and weak. The sight of his shaking hands and panicked expression sickened me.

Landmine strode over, sneered at the man cowering at my feet. "Thought there wasn't supposed to be any security."

Zeal crossed her arms. "Probably a manager. Still, the place is supposed to be empty."

Ultra flexed his hands. "Then let's make it so."

He stopped when I stood in front of him. "What's your problem?"

When he pushed forward, I shoved him back, bared my teeth. "He's just an old timer."

Landmine burst into laughter. "Oh, that's rich. The ruthless Overwhelm has a soft spot for senior citizens." Her eyes gleamed as she nudged her toe against the old man's leg. He whimpered, then screamed when she slammed her foot on his knee.

"Hey!" I grabbed her arm.

"You're the boss now?" Her voice pitched low. Dangerous.

"I'm not letting you hurt him."

"Then it's time you learned your manners. "

Ultra grabbed me from behind. Before I could break free, Zeal's fist slammed into my face, my stomach, my legs. My powers wavered, surging then retreating, already overspent from a night of fighting and hurting others. Pain exploded as Zeal crushed my foot.

I went down as the others closed in. Feet and fists slammed into me from every direction. Over the thud of them against my body, I heard the sound of Landmine's gleeful laugh, the old man's plaintive wails.

The memories faded. I found myself back in my studio apartment, staring at my hands. "The police found me and the manager. We were both messed up. Russel made it through, barely. Cassi stayed with me until I got better. She paid a lot of money for a good lawyer, a youth advocate, a counselor."

I swallowed, hard. "Not all of the security cameras were busted. The footage showed me trying to stop the others. We found a sympathetic investigator, and Russel testified on my behalf. I helped put away the gang's key players, got off easy. Did a lot of community service."

"Why did you stop them?" Briar asked.

I clenched my jaw. "One thing to fight people who want to fight. Beating an old man? It's fucked up."

"Yeah, it is. What happened to Russell?"

"Lives in Maui now. Raises chickens. He sends me Christmas cards."

She squeezed my hand, smiled. "You're a good man, Jase."

I glared. "I stole, committed violence. I beat the shit out of anyone who got in my way."

"You saved a helpless person. Put away bad guys. You remember his name. I'm not saying it makes up for the things you did. But I do think making amends counts."

"It's still there. Inside me." I shook my head. "I don't know if I have it in me to change. Not even for you."

She touched my cheek. "You already changed yourself. And you don't realize what a miracle that is."

She was the miracle. I'd given up my old way of life because I was sliding into a dark place. One where the lives of innocents didn't matter.

I might have hauled myself out of the pit, but Briar had drawn me into a place full of light and warmth.

I gathered her to me. Her lips met mine, her hands linking behind my neck. I kissed her back, gave myself the pleasure of touching her body. Her breathing quickened, her mouth eager.

I shoved up her shirt. One flick loosened her bra, spilling her breasts. I stroked my thumbs over her nipples, lowered my head to skim my teeth over the side of her neck, tasting her skin.

"More," I said.

33 LULLABY

I dragged at Jase's shirt, flung it to one side. My hands streaked over his shoulders, his chest. His warm skin was smooth, taut over honed muscles. The fine hairs trailing down the center of his abs tickled my palms. He smelled like soap and clean laundry and sexy male.

He groaned when I palmed his erection through his pants. Kneeling, he gripped the tops of my jeans, yanked them and my panties down with one fierce move. Leaving them bunched around my knees, he gripped my hips, holding me in place. His tongue delved into me, hot and slick.

I bucked, knees shaking. His mouth was hot, insistent. Determined to pleasure me. I tangled my fingers in his hair, yanked his head back.

He growled, glared at me. "I'm not done."

I kicked off my jeans, shoved at him until he lay on his back on the bed. Straddling him, I gave myself the pleasure of biting his neck, his shoulder, his strong jaw. "My turn."

I worked off his pants, bit my lip at the sight of his throbbing cock. I gave it one long, slow lick, savoring the taste.

Grabbing him by the base, I took him into my mouth. Let the tip nudge the back of my throat.

He groaned, his hand cupping the back of my head. His head fell back, the cords in his neck and shoulders straining.

Crawling up, I straddled him, positioned him at my entrance. His hands gripped my hips as I eased myself onto him. I shuddered at the deep invasion. Arched my back when Jase's thumbs flicked over my nipples. His intense gaze fixed on me as I rode him deep, grinding against him.

My hips moved at their own pace, the skin between my thighs growing damp. Our hitched breaths and moans filled the air, mixing with the sounds of rustling sheets and slapping skin.

My sex clenched, my belly tensing. "Coming."

"Do it. All over me."

I shattered, my entire body quaking. Waves of pleasure rolled through me, my head falling back as the orgasm tore through me.

Jase's hands braced my hips as he shoved into me at a furious pace. He moaned, his cock pulsed hard inside me, releasing himself.

I flopped on top of him, burrowing my face against the side of his neck. Cool air blew over my sweat-slicked skin. The sheets lay twisted around us. Even the fitted one had come untucked, the corner bunched under the pillows.

I cleared my throat. It was tight from breathing hard. And, well, other things.

Jase got up, returned with a glass of water. He passed it to me first, the cool liquid soothing my throat. Taking a swig for himself, he climbed in beside me. He hitched one of my knees, draping my leg over his middle. His other hand cradled the back of my head, held me close.

I sighed, burrowed in. "So much for talking like sensible adults."

He chuckled, a low throaty sound. "It's impossible around you."

"It's my fault?"

"Damn right it is." He pressed a kiss to the top of my head. "I can't keep my hands off you."

Thrilled, I let myself wallow in the warmth between us. "Thank you for sharing your past with me."

"It's not pretty."

"It's yours. I'm not giving you a bullshit line about it honing you into a fine man or whatever. I'm thanking you for trusting me."

"I do. As much as I trust anyone, at least."

Something crunched as I shifted. I reached under my butt, found a popped bag of chips. They must've escaped my bag in the tussling.

"Sorry, the crumbs." I yelped when he rolled me onto my back, licked at my bare thighs, my ticklish knees.

"Hm. Jalapeño." When I laughed, he smiled. With crinkly eyes and the dimple and everything.

Then, he got to work.

After, I was half dozing and basking in afterglow when a chime brought me around.

Jase shifted, untangling himself as he reached for his HC. He glanced at the screen, cleared his throat. "Audic respond. Alba, what's up?"

"Have you see Cassi? I can't get a hold of her."

Jase sat up. "What?"

"She was supposed to be here an hour ago. I called the other club, went by her apartment." Alba's voice tightened. "I can't find her."

"I'll call you back." Ending the call, he flicked open his messages.

I sat up, leaned in to rub his back. "Anything?"

"No— Wait." He flicked open a message, scanned it. His back stiffened, his eyes wide as he stared.

"Jase?" When he didn't respond, I leaned over to read.

PARKCASSILTD: I'm leaving. Sorry.

My heart sank. No explanation, no other messages, nothing.

Jase hadn't moved or responded. He sat, staring at nothing.

"Hey." I grabbed his hand, startled. His fingers were ice cold, his palm damp.

"It's my fault." His hands shook, his voice half-choked. "It's my—"

"Hey!" Setting my jaw, I gripped his shoulders, gave him a shake. "Snap out of it. We don't even know what's going on yet."

"You read it. She got tired of my bullshit and left. Just like our parents."

"Cassi loves you. She wouldn't abandon you."

"She has before."

I tensed, pulled back. "What?"

"In middle school. I got into a fight with some older kids, wrecked part of the school building. I waited in the detention center but she didn't come. I got home and she was gone."

He shuddered. "Days went by, weeks. I found out later she'd gone to New York. Wanted to start over without our parents, without me."

His gaze dropped to the bed. "She came back, but I always wondered if she regretted it."

My heart tightened at the thought of Jase as a boy, a child, sitting alone in a detention center. Had they put him in limiters? Had he been injured, afraid?

Another image of him at home. Waiting for family to come. Had there been food? Had someone, anyone, checked on him?

Terrified of the vacant look in his eyes, the bleak expression on his face, I wrapped my arms around his neck. "We don't know if that's what happened here."

"Then how do you explain this."

"Bad joke, a mistake, or she got lost, hell, I don't know. The Cassi I know wouldn't just leave you and Alba and her club." When he didn't respond, I pushed. "Maybe there was an accident. We'll contact the hospitals, the police."

Just don't give up, I added silently.

"Hospitals. Right." He scrubbed a hand over his face, let out a shuddering exhale. "Hospitals first."

We worked separately, contacting the various hospitals and clinics around Mayport, out in Jacksonville. I scoured the news, police reports, local Impulse feeds. Meanwhile, Jase put in calls to her contacts.

"No major accidents," I said when he hung up. "Public transportation's working normally."

"Nothing from her employees. Shit, where the hell did she go?"

I bit my lip. Was she really gone? Hard to picture Cassi just taking off without even dropping a pin.

"A pin," I murmured. "Let me see the message." I tapped it, opened up the details. Time stamp, her brand of HC, location.

Jase studied the text. "'Sent near Osprey Beach Park.'"

"Right by the institute. Hold on." I racked my brain. "Ashley. Dr. Singh's assistant. And another girl. Crap, who was it."

I opened a screen, did a search for the news article my uncle had sent me. "Here. 'Local girl goes missing. Last known location, Osprey Beach.'"

"You think someone there is kidnapping people?"

"Maybe. But we can't just go to a beach and look for creepers. Talk about needle in a haystack."

"The girl." He tapped the news story, expanding it to fill the screen. "Ashley and my sister we know. If she's also connected, we need to figure out how."

"It'll take time to get a special warrant."

His hands fisted, his jaw tight. "This is my sister we're talking about."

My stomach knotted. Technically, license candidates needed one to do investigations. It wasn't unheard of for us to do things on our own, of course. We're Powerhouses. We don't call the authorities, we charge in.

But I was worried about Jase. I'd always assumed him to be controlled, level-headed. Now, I realized it was only because he kept such a tight rein on himself. Because he was afraid of what would happen if he didn't.

If Cassi was in danger, how far would he go?

I grabbed his hand, squeezed. "Let's go."

We changed first, both of us silent. As we headed for the car, I made a silent promise to watch over him.

And to be with him, no matter what happened.

34 LULLABY

"Where to?" I asked, climbing into the passenger seat.
"The article said her brother is asking for clues to her whereabouts." As the car slipped into traffic, Jase opened the story on a screen, flicked it towards me.

"Deron Samuels, CEO of Icondustrial Technologies." I studied the man in the crisp suit. "Let's hope he's willing to speak to us."

I spent the ride going back through Cassi's Impulse feed, searching for clues. One of her recent posted photos made me pause. It was me and Jase at the bar of Iceberg. We looked close, happy.

Ace brought us a few blocks north of downtown, in the Faircrest district. Sleek, modern buildings speared towards the sky. The afternoon sun bounced off the shining towers of glass and steel, making me squint against the glinting light.

Skyrails glided over the streets and slid into the raised stations. People in suits lined up to board, speaking into earpieces, HCs, or to one another. Polished shoes and high heels clicked against the pavement. A food truck advertising

"Monster Burritos" did brisk business, the smell of carne asada filling the air.

Outside one of the buildings, a burbling fountain poured streams of water into a shallow pool. The building's logo shone through the falling water: Icondustrial Technologies.

The doors slid open and we entered a spacious lobby. A long roll of carpet led us to the front desk, the path lined on either side with dark green plants spearing out of fat black stones. Calming string music piped through unseen speakers. The air smelled of clean tiles and greenery.

At the front desk, a holoscreen shimmered to life as we approached.

"Welcome to the offices of Icondustrial Technologies. How may I help you?"

"Deron Samuels," Jase said.

"Do you have an appointment?"

"It's about his sister," I said. "Mona."

"I'm afraid Mr. Samuels is busy today."

I choked back the urge to call the computer a tight-ass. "Can you give him a message? We may be able to help him."

"Help with what?"

Jase and I turned at the sound of a new voice. A tall brown-skinned man walked through the front doors. He wore an immaculate navy blue suit and carried a bag from the burrito truck.

"Are you Deron Samuels?" I asked.

"I'm afraid we don't accept walk ins."

"It's about Mona."

"You knew my sister?"

"May we have a few minutes?"

Samuels studied us for a moment. "Jean, hold my calls."

I exhaled, relieved. Tight-Ass Jean gave her affirmative as we walked past the front desk.

"Ten minutes," Samuels said in the elevator.

The doors slid open, revealing a sprawling office floor. People in sharp business suits sat at cubicles, working at HC stations or talking on screens. The clean smell of circulating air mixed with the enticing scent of coffee. Holo-images lined the walls, morphing continuously into new pictures. Stock numbers, data, company announcements.

Samuels headed past the cubicles to a large corner office separated from the rest of the space by spotless glass walls. A long, sleek desk spanned the space. The smart surface lit as we entered, welcoming Mr. Samuels while displaying the time and an upcoming appointment.

"Two friends of ours are also missing," I said the moment the door closed.

"I'm sorry about your friends." Samuels set the takeout bag on the desk, closing the door and ordering the windows to shade. The glass walls tinted in acknowledgement. "You think it's connected to Mona."

"Our friends aren't the type to run off and leave. What about Mona?"

"My sister had difficulties adjusting as a teenager." His expression grew weary. "I wish she'd come to me first."

"Maybe she didn't have a choice," I said.

"You think this is an elaborate kidnapping scheme?" Samuels shook his head. "I ran a full investigation using my not insignificant resources. Even contacted the Bloodhound."

"The Bloodhound." Jase crossed his arms. "That's some connection."

"My family and hers are close. Mona and I are both latents."

"Latents," I said to Jase. "All three of them."

"Definitely a connection."

"I don't know if you two are on to something or if you're

chasing shadows."

"We won't stop looking," I said. I couldn't. Not until I knew Cassi was okay.

"If you find out anything," Samuels said as we exchanged info. "Call me."

"If it's criminal activity, it might be dangerous."

His eyes flashed, his voice lowering. "Certainly for the person who took my sister, it'll be dangerous indeed."

"Who'd want to kidnap latents?" I asked as Jase and I exited the building. "Someone with a fetish?"

"Or an agenda. Kidnapping people this close to the institute. We're lucky we noticed, but it would've been only a matter of time before someone did. They're either stupid or they're confident they'll get away with it."

"We need more to go on. There may have been other disappearances."

Jase glared at the ground. His shoulder muscles bunched, straining the fabric of his shirt.

I grabbed his hand, squeezed until he looked at me. "We're going to find them."

"What if they're—"

"Don't even think it." When he frowned, I glanced around. Spotted the food truck. "Hey, I'm starved. Let's get burritos. If CEO Guy eats them, I bet they're beyond."

He came along when I dragged him.

"Guac? Sour cream?" I asked.

"Sure."

"What about sauce? Mild, spicy, or surface of the sun?"

His lips tugged. "Spicy."

As we waited in line, I rubbed his arm. "We'll recharge, rest our brains, make a plan."

"And then?"

"Then we do what Powerhouses do. We kick ass."

35 STRONGHOLD

Loaded with burritos the size and density of boulders, we found a stone bench on the edge of a small park. Palm trees waved against the late evening sky. Smoke billowed from the food truck, carrying with it the smells of grilled meats and warmed tortillas.

Pedestrians filled the walkways. Business execs, students, clusters of tourists. Since the temperature hovered in the 60s, everyone was bundled for Arctic conditions. The sound of countless feet hitting the pavement made a rhythmic backdrop to the hum of public transportation.

I took a swig of neon bright Mexican soda. The sweetness hit me, a wash of sugar with the spike of fizz. "My sister and I fought before she disappeared. I told her about our fake arrangement."

Briar bit her lip. "Might not have anything to do with what's going on." When I said nothing, she exhaled. "Food first. Then we make a plan."

She peeled foil from her burrito, closed her eyes as she

savored the first bite. "Damn, this is good. You have a favorite food truck?"

"I don't eat much take out."

"So this is kind of living dangerously for you."

"Don't knock my nutrient shakes until you've tried them."

"With the guac and salsa, this is practically a salad."

"Guac's not a vegetable."

"Avocados are."

"Technically, they're a berry." When she narrowed her eyes at me, I laughed, the tension draining out of me. The lingering guilt from fighting with my sister eased, leaving me lighter.

It was easy to enjoy Briar's company. She was warm, open. She played video games in sloth pajamas.

When it was time to work, she didn't cut corners. Her notes for the project were well-thought out, carefully cited. She gave every ounce of herself when she put on her uniform.

Revealing my past to her left me hollowed out. I'd laid it at her feet to drive her away.

Rather than backing off, she'd reached out. Not in the way some craved a bad boy. But with understanding and compassion.

She crumbled the wrapper, made the two point shot into the closest recomposter. "Fuel accomplished. Now the plan."

"Talk to Dr. Singh. Find out more about Ashley. Hit the park, search for clues, witnesses." Unlikely with the previous cases, as they'd happened awhile ago. Still, perhaps someone had spotted Cassi.

"If others have also gone missing, we'll have more connections."

I considered. "We'll run a search on recent missing. Find out if any of them are reported latents."

"Latents." She started to say something else, stopped. Her back straightened, her brow furrowing.

"What?"

"Just thinking." She glanced at her HC. "I'm going to call my work place. Be right back."

She deeper moved into the park, spoke in a quiet voice through her HC. I tossed the garbage, stood watching the city while my mind drifted. Cassi's tight expression during our argument haunted me. If the last words I said to her were out of anger, I'd never forgive myself.

"You still blame yourself for what happened. You have to let go of that and live your life."

My sister's support had given me a second chance. I had to get her back. Whatever the cost.

Briar returned, frowning. "Can we stop by the arboretum." She shoved her hands into her jacket pockets. "I know we're on a job, but I'd like to go. Just for awhile."

I couldn't say no.

"Promise me you'll take care of yourself," she said on the drive over. "You're strong, invincible. Doesn't mean you get to take all the hits. Doesn't mean I'm not going to fight to keep you safe."

I wasn't sure where this was coming from, but I said, "I don't want you to get hurt."

"That's the same as not letting me live. You're my partner. The guy I'm crazy about." She hesitated, licked her lips. "I need to know you're in this with me. No more half-measures. I need you to trust me."

I studied her for a long moment. "Okay."

"Good." Her fingers drummed against her thighs before reaching for the in-dash earbud compartment. "I'm going to use one." She popped it into her ear, flipped her hair over it. "Hopefully I don't lose it. I'm always losing mine."

"You're nervous."

"Aren't you?"

"More pissed than anything." I ground my teeth. "I want my sister back. And I want the lowlives who took her to pay."

"If we don't find a lead, we'll call in big guns. Dr. Singh, your parents."

My parents. Would they respond? They'd always encouraged us to be independent, handle our own problems. A common mindset among PN parents.

Hell, I didn't even know where they were. If they were on a secret mission or responding to a crisis, it might be months, years before I heard from them.

Cassi and the other missing people didn't have that long.

Ace parked and we hoofed it the rest of the way. Fall break meant the campus was mostly empty. The pre-sunset light flooded the empty pathways, the only sound the rustle of wind through trees.

Briar led the way, taking us toward a small dock on the edge of the pond. The smell of fresh water filled the air. Waves lapped at the shore, the surface rippling.

"This is nice. Peaceful." Briar looked around, glanced at her HC.

I frowned. "What's with you?"

"Oh, she's nervous about introducing her boyfriend to me."

I spun, stared as Landmine emerged from a cluster of trees. Her gaze fixed on me, her lips peeled back in a predatory grin. "Then again, I already know you quite well. Don't I, Overwhelm?"

"What the hell." I fisted my hands, my power surging to the surface.

Small, soft fingers grabbed me. I stared at Briar, down to where she gripped my arm. A sharp sting bit into my skin. I felt the flare of her ability, the shift in my energy as she opened the current.

The world spun. I fell to my knees, my vision turning dark.

I fought to speak, to ask her why. My lungs were lead weights in my chest, my consciousness fading.

I hit the ground hard, a puppet with its strings cut.

Landmine laughed, the sound distant and muffled. "You should be used to getting betrayed."

The last thing I saw was Briar's pained expression. "I'm sorry."

Landmine emerged from the trees. Even as she goaded Jase, she sent me a quick, sly smirk.

I wiped my damp palms over my jeans, tried to steady my breathing. My pulse roared in my head.

Good thing Jase wasn't paying attention to me. Instead, he glared at Landmine, features tense.

"What the hell," Jase snarled, hands fisting. He started towards her.

No time to waste.

I grabbed his arm, my ability lighting under my skin. I had to be fast, put him under before he reacted. I opened the channel of energy between us, measured the right amount. Not too much, not too little.

This had to go perfectly.

He fell to his knees in front of me, his expression bleak. His eyes went from hard to glassy, losing their fury.

I swallowed against the burn in my throat. "I'm sorry," I whispered.

He hit the ground, hard enough to make me flinch.

Invincible or not, I hoped he hadn't cracked his head.

"I'm a bad guy and even I think that's cold."

I turned to Landmine, my blood boiling at the condescending look on her face.

Serena emerged from the trees, planted a fist on her hip. She glanced at Jase then back to me. "Doc's waiting."

"One minute." Landmine stalked over to Jase's body, nudged it with her boot.

I snarled. "What the hell are you doing?"

"Tying up lose ends." Grinning, she planted her foot against Jase's chest.

Her ability blasted him with the force of a cannon. It knocked him clear off the dock, out over the pond.

He hit the water, sending waves splashing the shore.

"Felt good." Dusting off her palmss, Landmine leered at me. Daring me to do something.

I bit my lip, temped down the rage flaring inside me. I wanted to plant my fist in her smug face.

I crossed my arms, hoped I appeared more irritated than concerned. "Finished?"

"Almost." She grabbed my arm, tore my HC from my wrist. "Can't have you changing your mind, calling for backup."

Throwing it to the ground, she hovered her hand over it. Concussive force blasted from her palm, smashed into my HC. It shattered into bits of glass and metal. The pretty rose quartz band crushed to powder.

I pressed my lips together, remembering my dad's face when he'd given me the band. The pride in his voice.

"Go out there and do some good, kid," he'd said to me.

I swallowed against the bitterness in my throat.

Serena turned away. "Let's go."

We got into Serena's car, me in the back. Most of the students had gone home for fall break. The institute stood eerily quiet, deserted. The building windows were dark, the lots empty of vehicles.

I took one glance through the back window, searching the lake's surface for any sign of movement.

Nothing.

Jase was tough, I told myself.

But he was out cold, another part of me whispered. Sleeping people can't swim.

I pressed my lips together hard, my entire body tense. Once again, I'd used my powers on Jase and abandoned him. This time, it might've cost him his life.

"Ready for a life of crime?" Landmine asked me.

"As long as I get what I was promised."

"That's the spirit. What's your handle? Not your lame-ass goody goody one. You'll want a new one for turning criminal."

I thought for a moment, then said, "Stunner."

"Not bad. Serena hasn't decided on one yet." Landmine rolled her eyes.

"You put too much importance on superficial shit," Serena muttered, swiping at a holoscreen.

"What's the fun of being a baddie if you don't do what you want?"

"I'm not in it for kicks like you."

Landmine glowered. I tensed, watching the two of them. Figured my new villainous cohorts had bad blood between them.

"Your sister." I met Serena's eyes in the rearview mirror. "You mentioned her before."

"I'm not telling you shit." The words came out tight, harsh.

Landmine howled, kicking back in her seat. "What a tight-ass."

We parked outside one of the social sciences buildings. The sun was just setting, turning the sky violet and orange.

A group of people clustered near the entrance. Talking, eating snacks, drinking Rocket water. Empty bags and cans littered the ground.

One of them, a pale, skinny boy wearing an AlterEgo t-shirt, straightened as we approached. "Boss."

Landmine answered. "Sonic. Anything to report?"

"It's been quiet."

"Boring," said a girl with light brown skin and a long, thick braid of dark hair. "Where's the action?"

"It's coming, Menagerie. Make sure you're ready."

"We will be," Sonic said.

Landmine punched him the arm, ruffled another kid's head.

As we moved past them, I studied their faces. Definitely a crew, and Landmine seemed to be in charge of them.

They were young, though. Teenagers. A couple of them looked even younger, like middle schoolers. Were they already villains? Wannabes? On the outside, they might pass for high schoolers checking out the campus. Not an unusual sight.

Still, where was campus security? Visitors passes or not, they were obviously loitering. Why hadn't they been rounded up?

I bit my lip, my shoulders tensing. The situation was getting more and more complicated.

We rode the elevator in silence, Landmine shooting me winks. I did my best to ignore her, to stay focused.

The elevators opened to one of the basement archives. Lights flared to life as we entered. Gleaming linoleum floors clicked underfoot. Rows and rows of shelves spanned into the distance, filled from end to end with filed documents.

A holoscreen on the wall churned through rows and rows of data at dizzying speeds. Some of the shelves had been cleared to make space for science equipment. Mini centrifuges, plastic packages of pipettes, micro fridges.

"Hey, doc!" Landmine called. "We brought her."

I moved to follow, stopped when Serena grabbed my arm.

"Not so fast. I don't trust you yet," she said, squeezing hard enough to hurt. "Stay where I can see you."

I shook her off. "I held my end of the bargain. I took care of Jase, gave you his sister. I sent a whole list of other latents we could grab today. What more do you want?"

Footsteps clicked against the tiles. "Conviction."

The voice made me freeze. My stomach twisted as I turned.

Dr. Linden emerged from behind a shelf. He gave me a sad smile. "You'll need it for what's to come."

37 STRONGHOLD

The cold water swallowed me. I sank, the world around me growing darker. My ability flared, desperate to keep me alive. But there was no one to fight, nothing to protect against.

Water flooded my nose, my mouth, poured down my throat. The world above grew dimmer, farther away.

Hands grabbed me. Hauled me toward the light. I had the vague sensation of being thrown onto the ground, my limbs dead weight.

"Is he alright?"

"God, did he drown?"

Pressure against my chest. Again and again. My lungs seized, forcing out water and bile. My throat spasmed, raw from the strain.

Fingers pressed against the side of my neck.

"Pulse is okay."

"The patch."

Someone peeled off the Extra Strength Insta-snooze patch stuck to my skin.

The second it was gone, my metabolism kicked in. That, plus the boost of energy Briar slipped me, fought to negate the medicine already in my system.

"Trying resuscitation." Hands clamped on either side of my head.

I forced my eyes to open. Hector's face stopped an inch from mine, his lips parted.

I coughed. "Back off, Diaz."

He blinked, then grinned. "Hey, he's awake."

Tristan, Lucie, and Hazel's faces appeared over Hector's shoulders, all of them in their uniforms. Though the special body suit remained dry, Tristan's hair was soaked, clinging to his scalp. He must've been the one to dive in after me.

Hazel shoved Hector out of the way and leaned in close. "Okay?"

I sat up, rubbed my head. Pressure built behind my temples, sending throbbing pain through my skull. "I'm okay."

"Lucky we got here before you drowned," Hector said. "You coughed up water for awhile."

"Briar pinged us and dropped a pin," Lucie said. She pulled up a screen, flipped it around.

LULLABY: PB SANDWICHES 2NITE DINNER

"About peanut butter sandwiches?" Hector asked.

"It's our code for "Plan B," Hazel said. "Means 'I'm in trouble and bring back up.'"

I raked back my wet hair. I was freezing, my limbs numb and shaking. The taste of pond water saturated my senses. My stomach jumped, shuddered. It was like waking with a hangover.

I climbed to my feet. "They took her."

Lucie gasped. Beside her, Tristan crossed his arms, his expression grim.

"You know where?" Hazel asked.

I almost said no before remembering Briar's weird behavior.

"Hopefully I don't lose it."

I flicked open an HC screen, activated the app connecting me to Ace. A bird's eye view map of the city appeared. After a moment, a small green dot glowed on the screen. "There."

"You're tracking her?" Hector's brow arched.

"Earbuds from my car. She's wearing one. Let's move."

We piled into my car, Tristan, Hazel, and Hector squeezing into the back. I took the front seat, my focus on the screen in front of me.

"Where to?" Lucie asked, slipping into the passenger seat.

I brought up a screen with a map, zoomed in on the signal.

Hazel wormed between the seats. "The institute."

"Criminal PNs with a hideout on campus?" Lucie shook her head. "How's that possible?"

"They're working with someone." I said. "Got to be. My bag in the back. There's fuel."

Hazel rummaged in the trunk, returned with a backpack. She dug around in it, passed me a nutrient bar, peanut butter flavored, and a water. She passed more to the others, took some for herself.

We fueled while the car sped across campus.

"Who are we up against?" Hector asked, gnawing his way through two bars at once.

"At least one criminal PN." I outlined what I knew about Landmine. "There'll be more on scene. She always ran with a crew. And we still don't know who's pulling the strings or why."

I chased the bar with the water, grabbed one of my

bodysuits from the compartment I kept onboard. "I'm going to change."

Hazel leaned forward, eyes wide.

"Hey!" she yelled when Hector hauled her back. "Rude."

"You're playing voyeur and I'm the rude one?"

While they tussled, Tristan pressed against the door, attempting to make his big frame as small as possible. Lucie cleared her throat and folded her hands in her lap before staring politely out the window.

I climbed out of my wet clothes and into the suit, thinking of Briar. The look on her face as she'd put me under. She'd known about the trap, helped to set it. Just enough, presumably, to get Landmine to trust her. She'd even sent an SOS to the others.

So why hadn't she told me?

"Together or nothing."

She'd obviously thought this through. She was smart, strong. It was on to me to trust her and the plan she'd come up with.

I exhaled, rolled my shoulders. Between the fuel and the burst of energy from Briar, my body was humming. Ready for a fight.

"Chat only. No vocals," I said. The others nodded, expressions grim.

The car stopped near one of the social science buildings. Sunset had long passed, plunging the campus into darkness. Lamps set at regular intervals poured light onto the walkways, leaving patches of deep shadows.

I parked at a distance and we moved closer on foot, stopping near an annex to study the main entrance. Signs of movement near the doors suggested a guard of some kind.

I met Hector's eyes, gave him a signal. He nodded and flashed out of existence.

I opened an HC screen to its smallest size, adjusting the light so it was barely illuminated. The others did the same, joining the group chat I started. Minutes passed while we waited, holding our breaths.

A gust of wind, a slight pop of sound, and Hector appeared. His fingers moved over his screen.

HECTIC: Lights in the ground windows. Basement? Three at front doors, two at side entrance. They look like kids, man.

INCOGNITO: Basement's going to be hard to sneak into. Fewer points of entry.

PURLOIN: Plan?

STRONGHOLD: When in doubt? Surprise and overwhelm.

38 STRONGHOLD

STRONGHOLD: Hector, draw the two side guards. Make enough ruckus to pull the front ones.

HECTIC: My specialty.

STRONGHOLD: Hazel, go with him. Use caution. We don't know what their abilities are. Lose or immobilize them, then join us. The rest of us make for the entrance.

We closed our screens. Hector was gone in an instant, folding in on himself in a flicker of light and sound. Hazel followed, shimmering out of view like a mirage.

We waited, keeping low and quiet.

Shouts. Footsteps running. A whoop followed by a crashing sound, metal against metal.

I signaled the others, taking the lead.

We rounded the building, paused at the entrance. Empty soda bottles and bags of chips littered the ground, left by the lookouts. I heard them in the distance shouting and swearing.

I tried the door. Locked. I turned to Lucie.

She nodded, then focused on the door, her hand flexing.

Metal squealed, bent. The lock disappeared from the door frame, folding in on itself. It reappeared in Lucie's hand, intact.

I nudged the door open, waited. No alarms, no sound of movement.

Signaling the others, I lead the way inside.

Silence. The building lobby stood quiet and empty. We crept across the marble flooring, keeping to the shadows. Hallways branched off, leading to offices, classrooms.

My patience wore thin. I wanted to bust through walls, smash things until I forced the captors out of hiding. But Briar and Cassi's lives depended on me keeping my head.

I opened a new chat.

STRONGHOLD: Another basement beneath this one. Then the archives.

PURLOIN: Split up?

I considered. It'd make the search faster, but we had no idea what we were up against. Plus the noise outside might draw more guards.

Safety in numbers.

STRONGHOLD: Stay together for now.

We took the stairs to the first basement. Lucie stopped at the door, pressed her ear to it. She frowned, leaned back.

A loud whine of sound filled the air, crescendoed. The door began to vibrate.

"Down!" I ordered.

We threw ourselves to the floor as the door exploded off its hinges. The walls rattled, the metal stairs groaned. An overhead light shattered, plunging the alcove into darkness. Shrill echoes bounced around the room, vibrating through my skull, loud enough to rattle my teeth.

A kid, barely a teenager, stepped through the doorway, wearing an AlterEgo shirt that left his arms bare. He drew in a deep breath.

An enormous shadow leaped between us. The figure of an armored knight towered high. Blood ran in thick, sludgy rivers, coating the silvery surface. He hefted the monstrous sword.

Ego-shirt took one look at Tristan and recoiled. He turned to flee. "Intru—"

Lucie tackled him to the ground. As he struggled, she wrapped herself around him in a brutal leg and arm lock.

"Sonic?" A girl appeared at the end of the hall. Seeing us, she yelled, broke into a run. Halfway to us, she shape-shifted. A rhino burst through her skin, pebbled grey body filling the corridor. Bellowing, it lowered its head and charged.

Tristan threw himself forward. He slammed his sword into the scabbard on his back, braced for impact.

The rhino hit him dead on, pushing him backwards. Tristan gripped the animal by the horn and the forehead, feet gouging into the tiles as he fought to stop its momentum. Their struggle made the flooring shudder, the walls shake.

I moved towards him to help. Froze when I felt the shudder traveling through my body like a slow moving earthquake.

A burst of concussive force hit the broken door, sending it hurtling straight at Lucie.

I dashed for her, arms hooking around her and the kid, tackling the two of them into the stairwell. The door hit the empty doorframe behind us, slamming to a halt.

The three of us hurtled down the stairs. I gritted my teeth, fought to control my fall so I didn't land on top of them.

We landed at the bottom in a heap. Breathing heavy, Lucie staggered upright, stumbled.

A voice rasped in the darkness. "Good to see you, Overwhelm."

A booted foot came down on my hand. My power surged, saving my fingers from being crushed. I grabbed the ankle in front of me and yanked.

Landmine hit the stairs, the metal ringing as she landed. Screaming, she kicked out, freeing herself. I loomed over her, pulled back a fist.

She threw out a hand. Concussive force exploded from her palm, blasted me right in the face.

It was like getting hit by a battering ram. If my powers had been any less, my skull would've been crushed.

Even my ability didn't block the blow one hundred percent, maxed out like blown speakers. Blood poured from my nose, my ears, my mouth. My eyes teared, my throat burned raw from my own howl of pain. I fought to stay conscious, senses reeling.

Landmine's foot kicked me square in the chin. I fell to one side, my mouth flooding with blood. Dizziness racked me, leaving me no idea if I was standing or lying down. I retched, spat out one of my teeth.

"You'll regret betraying me." Landmine's words sounded muddy and far away. She lifted her hand.

Lucie tackled Landmine around the knees. The blast meant for me shot toward the ceiling, slamming into the tiles. The stairwell light exploded, the bulb swinging free before crashing to the floor.

Both of them went down. Landmine swore, throwing fists. Lucie gave as good as she got, expression focused as she fought

Landmine's wild swings with calm, precise blocks and quick blows.

"I got this. Go!" she yelled when I hesitated.

I climbed to my feet, started towards the next basement. I found the kid, Sonic, crouched in the next landing.

When I drew closer, he cringed back. Tears streaked down his cheeks. "It hurts. Hurts, hurts, hurts!" He clawed at his own throat, rocking back and forth. His nails gouged into his own skin, drawing blood.

He didn't seem injured. More like panicked. I grabbed him by the shoulder. "Hey, kid."

"Hurts, hurts," he wheezed. His mouth spasmed, his eyes rolling.

Gritting my teeth, I pulled back and slugged him.

He hit the ground, unconscious. I checked his breathing, found it evening out. I set him against the wall and continued down the stairs.

The second basement was dark and quiet. Faint light glowed at the end of the hall. I moved through the foyer, heading for the light, keeping low and silent.

Pausing in the door, I knelt, took a quick glance before pulling back. Not seeing or hearing anything, I rose, moved into the room.

It was a lecture space, the chairs stacked to one side in a haphazard tower. The tables lined one wall, surfaces covered with medical supplies. Syringes in plastic wrap, test tubes filled with clear liquid, IV bags. The air smelled of antiseptic and blood.

The light came from a row of stasis chambers. Nearby machines pulsed with lights and low beeping sounds.

I moved forward, examined the chambers. They were the kind used most often for mortally wounded PNs, putting them in deep cryosleep until they could be healed. I recognized Ashley and Mona in two of them.

My sister lay in the last one.

"Cassi." I pressed my palm to the surface. She lay still, her features cast blue by the chamber's internal lights.

Shaking, I struggled to stay calm. My instinct was to tear the chamber apart. But I had no idea what condition they were in. Forcing them out of cryosleep might endanger their lives.

For the moment, they seemed alive and intact. I needed to find Briar. Face whomever was behind this.

"I'll be back." Promise made, I ran for the door. The only floor left was the archives. I leaped the stairs in one jump, boots ringing against the metal landing. I had to believe Briar was down there. Had to believe she was okay.

That I would get to her in time.

39 STUNNER

"You don't seem surprised," Dr. Linden said.

"Your research on latency. The paper I wrote about my family. I practically handed Serena the information about Cassi." I fisted my hands. "You know I work at the hospital, so you told Serena to approach me."

"Well done, Briar. I'd expect nothing less from you."

My stomach sank. This was a man I'd admired, trusted. I'd encouraged him to date my roommate, for God's sake.

When I'd realized the connection, I'd reached out to him, to Serena. Offered to bring in more latents.

The condition that I take out Jase had been the curveball. No doubt orchestrated by Landmine for the sake of revenge. Ultimately I trusted Jase to make it through and for Plan B to go into effect.

Though Linden's praise sickened me, I held my tongue. Until I found where they were keeping Cassi and the others, I had to play it smart.

"She says you made a bargain with her," Serena said, crossing her arms.

"Briar's going to join us. In exchange, I'm going to grant her a wish."

Landmine snorted. "Glass slippers?"

Linden frowned. "Join your crew on standby."

Landmine scowled then stalked out of the room.

"She's too unpredictable," Serena muttered. "We need to cut her and those faultbags she recruited loose."

"We need them for the process." Linden gave me an apologetic look. "They're a necessary evil, I'm afraid."

"My uncle," I said. "You said you can give him abilities."

"That's the beauty of it. He already has them. Lying dormant in his genes, waiting to be awakened." He walked to me, his features gentle. "I can do that for him. For all latents."

"Why the subterfuge? I'd think latents would line out the doors for a chance."

He crossed over to wallscreen, stared at it. The endless scrolling numbers reflected against his glasses, hiding his eyes. "There are costs. Nothing comes free. The process, I'll admit, is a long and painful one. We're honing the effects to be permanent, however at the moment, they're temporary. Not entirely controllable. Some simply don't respond to the procedure, no matter how many attempts. I'm sure you agree the chance is worth it."

"I don't trust her." Serena crossed her arms. "She's a classic Powerhouse. Too much do-gooder in her."

"One person becomes two becomes many. This is how we're going to convince the public that what we're doing is viable." He said it with a patient, firm tone that told me they had the same argument multiple times.

"I want to help my uncle," I said.

"You're a shitty liar," Serena said.

Linden chuckled, adjusted his glasses. "Let's give her the tour. Then we'll know for certain."

I followed him deeper into the archives. Serena tailed us, keeping close behind me. I could tell she was waiting for an excuse to take me out.

Past the shelving lay other corridors. Autolights triggered, the fluorescent bulbs flickering to life. We trod over cold white linoleum, past emptied rooms and vacated offices.

"You were one of my first considerations for partners when I began my research," Linden said. "You can't imagine my pleasure when you contacted me. Your ability makes you uniquely qualified to help us."

"Who's 'us?'" I asked.

"I say 'us' but we're mostly a one man operation at the moment."

"Why Landmine? I get the need for muscle, but she's volatile."

"I can't say why, but the Patron chose her himself."

The Patron. I filed the name away in my memory.

"Did you know," he continued, tone conversational. "This building used to be a science center, before being converted to a humanities department. Much of the equipment was removed, but there were many useful items in storage."

He stopped beside a wide window, the autoshading activated to hide what was in the room. "It's been convenient for our process."

He flipped the switch, the glass shifting to clear.

My blood ran cold.

Children. Not teens like Landmine's crew. Little kids. The oldest, a slim boy with dark brown skin and braids, looked maybe eight. The youngest, a girl with wispy blonde hair and pale skin, seemed five at the most.

There were close to a dozen of them, all wearing hospital scrubs. Bright primary colors decorated the room. Cheerful rainbow wall decals, smiling suns, plump animals. Most of them played with toys or flipped through picture books. Not holo ones, actual paper books.

"What the hell is this?" My voice shook.

"Our latest batch. They're latents. Like me, like your uncle. Their potential waiting to be unleashed."

"They're children."

"Young people make the best subjects. Their bodies are malleable, able to recover from the effects of genetic encouragement."

"By 'encouragement,' I'm guessing you don't mean pep talks."

"We extract the materials from older latents, use them to create the booster serum. There are many specifics, some of which I don't understand myself. Essentially, we encourage those dormant abilities to awaken."

He surveyed the children like a proud father. "That's what I'm calling it. 'Awaken.' With it, I'll usher in a new age for latents."

Nausea rolled through me, twisting my insides. I swallowed against the bitter tang in my mouth. "This is fault on so many levels."

"You're not convinced. It's understandable. I was the same initially. I've come to view it as a necessary sacrifice."

Gorge rose in my throat. I tried to remember the mission, to keep my facade But the sight of those kids enraged me.

"Performing experiments on unwilling people you've kidnapped is fault no matter how you spin it."

He fixed me a hard stare. "If this hasn't convinced you, then I'm afraid nothing will."

"Don't I get a chance to prove myself?"

"Fair enough. Drawing latent abilities takes quite a toll on our subjects. You're going to use your power to sustain one while I pull samples."

I pressed my lips together. Imagined Cassi being tapped, like a damn maple tree. Her life literally pumped into some unsuspecting kid.

The piece in my ear chirped, synching to Ace.

Jase was close.

"What the hell was that?" Serena grabbed my shoulder, shook me. My hair fell back from my face.

She snatched the earbud, threw it to the ground, stomped on it. "You fucking—"

I moved first. Slammed my elbow back into her sternum. When she doubled over, I brought my knee up, aiming for her nose.

She dodged the kick, shoving my knee to one side. "You bitch!" She bulled into me.

We hit the ground struggling. I hooked my legs around her knees, tangling us together long enough to use my ability. I slapped my palms to either side of her face, opened the dam.

Snarling, she grabbed my hands. Her nails dug into me, raking my skin. By then, however, my ability had done its work. Her energy poured into me. Usually, I carefully controlled the stream to keep from draining too much.

Now, safety measures didn't apply.

She keeled over on top of me, knocked out. I shoved her off, my body vibrating with her energy.

I scrambled to my feet, went into a defensive posture. Linden stood watching me, unmoved.

"Your powers would've been exceptionally useful to us," he said. "Landmine's followers are willing test subjects, but my dream is to bestow abilities to all worthy latents."

"And who gets to decide who's worthy and who gets siphoned? You?"

"Sacrifices must be made. It's a shame you don't understand."

"You've got kids locked up, you're torturing people, and I'm the shame?"

"Make no mistake, Briar." He removed his glasses, set them to one side. "I've put my money where my mouth is."

His flesh rippled, undulating and churning. His shirt buttons burst, the sleeves ripping apart. His muscles grew, ballooning out, stretching his skin until I feared it would burst. His height and width grew until he loomed over me.

He flexed his huge fists, stared down at me. "Allow me to show you just how far I'm willing to go."

40 STUNNER

I reeled, my lungs seizing at the sight. He hadn't just become bigger and stronger. His proportions had mutated. His neck and head were huge, his knuckles dragging the ground. He was like a primordial humanoid, his flesh stretched to the maximum, shoulders and arms bulging.

His muscles shifted and slid under his skin as though they were creatures trapped under a tarp. His head jerked and twitched like a broken doll's, his fingers twisting and bending before snapping back into place.

My flesh crawled. Whatever experiment used to give Linden this ability seemed unstable. His body kept twisting and readjusting as if it couldn't decide on a shape.

A thin line of drool escaped the corner of his lips, his words slurring as though his teeth were too big for his mouth. "You don't know what it's like. Watching your loved one suffer and die while you stand there, helpless."

His fiancee. Was that what lead him down this path?

"You're right, I don't." I clenched my fists. "I do know what

it's like to have a loved one kidnapped and tortured by a
professor I admired and tru—"

Roaring, he tackled me, his speed so fast all I could do was
brace for impact. We hit the ground, the air rushing out of me.

Linden straddled my middle, wrapped his massive fingers
around my neck. I struggled, kicking and punching, trying to
break his hold.

"Linden, wake up! I'm your student." I choked out the
words, hoping they'd reach him.

"The Patron said sacrifices are necessary."

"He's using you. You're a pawn." I had no idea of it was
true, but I wanted the professor to keep talking. Any chance to
distract him might give me a opportunity to break free.

"If the experiment succeeds, we can more than double the
number of PNs. Who knows what powers we might find lying
dormant."

His grip tightened, his thumbs gouging into my throat. "No
more deaths. No more tragedies."

My lungs seized, my mouth working as I struggled to
breath. Desperate, I fought hard. My nails raked his skin,
leaving bloody claw marks.

His brows drew together. Tears streamed down his cheeks,
dripped from his chin. "I was there and I couldn't save her. She
died while I watched, helpless. Why can't you understand?"

My vision faded, stars bursting against black. Another
moment and I'd pass out, then be killed by my sociology professor.

Not happening.

Gritting my teeth, I wedged my hands between his arms
then shot them to either side, pushing his elbows out.

He collapsed, his hold loosening. I slammed my head up,
smashing my brow right into his nose. Howling, he fell away.

I scrambled to my feet, sucking in great gasps of air.

Coughing, my throat raw from being crushed, I brought my fists in front of me in a defensive posture. "I understand you've completely lost your shit."

Linden snarled, the sound wet and muffled. Blood streamed from his nose, coating the bottom of his face, dribbling down his neck. He charged me again.

This time, I was ready. I ducked under his outstretched arms, punching my right fist into his groin, my left into his sternum.

He spun away, doubled over. I leaped onto his back. I'd prefer to say like a ninja or a panther, but at the moment I was more enraged spider-monkey. Wrapping my legs around his waist, I hooked one arm around his neck, my other hand grasping him by the nape as I unleashed my ability.

He snarled, tried to shake me loose. Spinning, he slammed back against the wall, crushing me between himself and the concrete.

Screaming in both rage and pain, I tightened my hold, willed the channel open wider. His energy poured into me, suffusing my blood. I felt lit from the inside out, my blood rushing through my veins so fast my pulse started to skip, my organs struggling to keep up.

He stiffened before his eyes rolled into his head. He crashed to the floor, throwing me clear.

I rose in time to see his body return to normal. He deflated, the skin going slack, the muscles shrinking.

I staggered, struggling to remain on my feet. My pulse fluttered, my skin broke into a cold sweat. The professor's energy coursed through me, way more than I'd expect from a latent. I vibrated from it, my limbs jerking.

And it had a strange feel to it. Crawly and prickly. Not right.

Was it because of the treatments? What the hell kind of weird experiments had they been running?

I fought to steady myself. An investigation could wait. Ideally, for someone way more qualified than me. I needed to get out, find help for those kids. My lungs heaving, I staggered over to the door.

It slammed open as I reached it. I braced for a fight.

Jase filled the doorway, stopping short. His face was bloody, his expression fierce, his hair wild.

At the sight of him, my knees threatened to buckle. "You're alive."

His features tightened. His arms hooked around my waist as he caught me in a fierce hug. "I'm the one who's relieved."

Hearing the strained relief in his voice, I hugged him back. "I'm okay."

He gave me a hard squeeze. Pulling back, he scanned my body, frowned at the blood on my forehead.

Chuckling, I stopped him by placing my palm over his heart. "I'm okay," I repeated. "Blood's not mine."

He relaxed. His gaze shifted to behind me. "Is that—"

"It is. I'll explain later. There are people who need help."

He straightened, nodded. "Let's go."

We hurried out of the basement to the staircase. My boots slapped against the metal steps, the sound ringing against the walls.

"The others?" I asked.

"Dealing with the crew." His expression tightened. "Including Landmine."

I scowled. "I've got something for her."

"Not if I get to her first."

"First come, first serve."

"A challenge, huh?" He gave me a cocky smirk. "Bring it on."

I grinned. It felt good, knowing he trusted me in a fight. And that I could trust him. "I love you."

We both froze in place. Jase stood several steps above me. He turned, body tense. "What?"

I gave a nervous laugh, my palms clammy. "Wow, that just came out. Not a great time." My face burned, from the bottom of my neck to my hairline.

I shook my head, started climbing the stairs again. "Forget it. We need to go."

His hand shot out, grabbed my arm. Now I was a couple steps above him. It evened out our heights, put us at eye level. My heart knocked when I saw the intense look in his eyes.

"No way I'm forgetting it." When I trembled, he cupped my face in his wide, warm palms.

The urge to touch him, to be touched, was a fire in me. My hands roamed his shoulders, his chest. Stroked his jaw, his hair. He was here and he was mine.

He rested his brow against mine. "Briar."

Tears burned the backs of my eyes. There was so much to say, so much to feel.

Shouts and crashes from above drew my attention. I glanced at the top of the stairs, saw flashing shadows and heard grunts of pain. Definitely a fight going on.

We turned back to one another. I sighed, smiled. "Let's go."

Jase nodded, gave my hand one last squeeze. A silent promise.

Side by side, we charged into the fray.

41 STRONGHOLD

We emerged from the staircase and into chaos.

Three of Landmine's crew teamed up on Lucie. Powers flared, fists flew. Lucie moved fast, dodging while dealing blows, using her ability to bring objects to her and then hurling them at anyone who came near.

Tristan and Landmine fought hand to hand. Landmine's ability smashed into the silver armor each time she punched, riddling it with dents. Tristan withstood the blows, his slow speed making his sword useless.

Lucie spotted us. "Briar! You're okay!"

Landmine whirled, fixed me a furious glare. "Not for long."

She charged me. I dodged her first blow, letting the blast of concussive force sail past. It hit a shelf, shattering it to splinters and sending books and pages flying.

I swung down on her outstretched arm, hitting her right in the elbow. "That's your problem, Lydia. You don't think before you act."

She snarled, her arm hanging limp at her side. "It's Landmine!"

When she kicked, I caught her foot, sent her toppling. Dodged another concussive blow. It burst right beside my ear, sending shockwaves of pain echoing through my head. A high-pitched whine filled my senses.

As I staggered, Lydia got to her feet, turned her palms to me.

Briar's foot kicked her right in the ribs. When Lydia fell, Briar was on her, hands around the other woman's neck. "Leave my boyfriend alone, you bitch!"

Lydia managed one choked gurgle before falling unconscious.

"You got to her first," I said, helping her stand.

"You got the first hit." She quivered, her fingers moving as if playing an invisible piano.

Too much energy, I realized. She was riding at maximum, her body fighting to control the extra input.

Tristan had joined Lucie, knocking out the last of the crew. Lucie had found a roll of duct tape, wrapped it around the group of teenagers.

Tristan's armor vanished, leaving him in his bodysuit. He straightened, exhaled, his skin coated with sweat.

"Hope that's the last of them," Lucie said.

Footsteps on the stairs. We braced.

Hazel and Hector rushed in.

"Briar!" Hazel ran forward, hugged her friend. "You're okay."

Briar grinned as Lucie joined the two of them in a group hug. "Y'all came."

"Of course we did."

"There are kids below," said Briar. "They need help."

"HCs aren't working," said Hector. "Must be some kind of blocker."

"Let's go outside."

"Wait." The sound of Tristan's low voice made us freeze.

He stood, facing the doorway leading to the sub basement, frowning.

He tensed. "Something's coming." In a flash, the bloody armor shot out of his skin and slammed into place around him.

A giant exploded through the doorway. Splintered wood and shattered concrete rained on us, the walls crumbling before its mammoth strength. It swung boulder sized fists, grunting as it bulled into the room.

It hit Hector like a wrecking ball, sending him flying. Hector hit the far wall, plowed clear through it, leaving a massive hole behind.

Hazel backpedaled. "What the hell is that?"

"It's Linden," Briar said, expression grim.

I stared at the monster. Though the features were distorted, there was some familiarity in the face.

It was enormous. Whatever mutation overtaking his body had swollen him to gargantuan size. Tristan's height barely reached his sternum, his limbs big around as tree trunks. The giant towered over us, a mythic creature of sinew and muscle.

Muscles that seemed alive. They rippled under his skin, sliding and trembling.

"It's him," Briar said. "He was experimenting on himself."

Lucie covered her mouth. "Owen."

"Stay alert," I said, injecting authority into my voice. The man was our enemy now.

The giant whirled on us, fists swinging. He smashed through shelves, shattered screens into glass shards. Walls exploded into splinters and dust.

Tristan met Linden head on, sword held flat in front of him as a barricade. The two met in a rushing fury of metal and muscle.

"Now," I yelled. "Surround him."

We rushed in. Lucie leaped onto Linden's back, her fists a flurry of punches. Hazel and Briar aimed for the ribs on either side. I joined in, dealing strikes to the kidneys, the liver, the spleen.

It wasn't enough. Whatever was pumping through Linden's veins made him impervious to our attacks. We were like wolves attacking a T. rex, dealing damage but not nearly enough.

Linden flung Lucie off his back and struck out to either side. He knocked Hazel and Briar away, smashed his fist straight down on Tristan. The big knight went to his knees, sword braced against Linden's blow.

Gritting my teeth, I swung over Tristan's head, aiming for Linden's throat. It was like punching an oak. The giant gurgled, his free hand smashing into me from the side. I hit the far wall, came to a stop.

Briar raced over to me, helped me sit up. "You okay?"

I pushed to my feet. "It's not enough. We need a more powerful hit."

Briar set her jaw. "Then we'll give him one." She grabbed my arm.

Energy flowed into me, flooded my bones, my blood. My body overflowed with heat like a star. Every cell, every drop of blood infused, lit up.

I caught her as she staggered, held her to me. "Fuck's sake," I said, wanting to argue with her decision.

Too late. Her head lolled, her eyes shutting.

A scream made me look up. Linden had Tristan pinned against the ground, his other hand clutching a furious Lucie. Hazel wrenched on the giant's fingers, trying to free her friend.

Tristan gripped the giant's wrist, struggled to push him off. His armor squealed as the metal plates ground together. He bellowed as his chest plate caved in under Linden's weight.

The floor beneath him sank, the tiles shattering into shards.

Dust billowed into the air. The crater deepened as Linden leaned his weight onto Tristan's body. Old, dark blood oozed from the armor, filling the cracks in the floor.

I laid Briar down and straightened. The strength from everyone she'd drained coursed through me. My blood pounded, my heart raced, air rushed into my lungs. My well of power filled and overflowed, my ability crescendoing to untold heights. I felt like I could run ten marathons, bench press an airplane.

Beat the shit out of a mutated giant.

Charging, I barreled into Linden's elbow. He crashed forward on top of Tristan, losing his grip on Lucie.

I was on him in a flash, striking with all my speed, all my power. One of my blows slammed him right in the eye.

He staggered sideways off Tristan. Enraged, he flailed, limbs striking out. One hit Hazel in the side, slammed her right into Lucie. The two went flying, hit the wall.

I dodged as Linden's fist came down. It smashed into the floor, shattering tile and leaving cracks in the concrete. He yelled as he swung, his breath blowing into my face.

Breathing heavy, spitting out a mouthful of dust, I braced for another attack.

A pop of sound and light. Hector appeared in the air near the ceiling, his face a mask of grim determination.

He fell from the sky, dropped down on the back of Linden's neck like a bird of prey.

Linden crashed face first into the floor. Gurgling, he swayed, pawed at the air, his features bloody.

Roaring, I focused my power into my fist and smashed it into the side of his head.

He hit the wall, cracking through the drywall and slamming into the steel stud beyond. Reeling, he gave one last moan before sliding to the floor and going still.

Hector staggered to his feet, coughed and waved at the dust clouds hanging in the air. "He's out? For real?"

Hazel swiped at her cheek, gave Linden a tentative nudge with her foot. "I think so."

Lucie cradled Tristan's head in her lap. He lay unconscious, mouth slack, his armor vanished. The wounds and blood remained. Every inch of him was soaked in red.

"It's bad," Lucie said, brows knitted. "He needs help."

"Why the hell aren't alarms going off?" Hector said.

"They must've cut them. Even the fire ones." I turned to him. "The security station."

When Hector teleported out, I said to Hazel, "Round the criminal PNs, secure them until help arrives."

"I'll help." Lucie set Tristan down gently before leaving with Hazel.

I scooped up Briar. Her skin was freezing. I held her close, willed my warmth into her.

Her eyes rolled as she forced them open. "Are we winning?"

I had to smile. "Yeah."

She clutched my shirt, lids drifting closed. "I keep breaking my promise to you. So fault."

"Technically, you only promised not to drain me."

"You're making excuses for me. Sweet."

"We're still going to have a long talk about it later."

She managed a laugh before going limp in my arms.

42 STUNNER

Two voices reached me as I woke, both familiar.

"This is ridiculous. Why isn't this room better equipped?"

A quiet chuckle. "This is a state of the art PN adapted wing."

"Medieval's what it is."

A surprised laugh bubbled in my throat, emerged as a ragged grunt. I forced my eyes to open. Faces hovered above me.

Uncle Brian frowned, brows furrowed. "Briar. You wake up right this second, young lady."

"Better do what he says. He's got the doctors terrified."

"Dad," I croaked. "Uncle Brian."

They looked similar, enough to tell they were brothers. Uncle Brian appeared more polished, with his trim haircut and shaven chin. My father's face was more weather worn from years of outdoor landscaping work. His eyes crinkled, his chin sporting a day's worth of scruff.

"Hey, kiddo," he said.

"She's crying. Are you in pain? These inept doctors—"

"Relax. She's just happy we're here." My dad winked at me.

"Of course we're here. Where the hell else would we be?"

I blinked through the tears, my vision blurring before coming into focus. Hospital lights overhead. Metal rails on either side of me. Over the sharp sting of antiseptic, the soothing scent of flowers. A machine beeped in the distance at a slow, rhythmic pace.

The blinds had been lifted, allowing golden afternoon light to pour into the room. A pale pink quilt lay over me, embroidered with fluffy white sheep. I recognized it as my childhood blanket from home.

My uncle and my dad stood on either side of my bed, hands on mine. Uncle Brian frowning while my dad had his usual placating expression. I hadn't seen him since the summer. The sight of his sun-tanned features and the touch of his rough hand warmed me through.

"Thanks for coming," I said, trying to swallow. My mouth was bone dry.

My dad picked up a glass of water from the side table, pointed the straw towards me. "You focus on getting better," he said while I drank.

Maybe it was the close calls, the recent fighting, the talk of latents. I found myself saying, "I'm sorry, Uncle Brian. That I manifested abilities instead of you."

Brian recoiled. "What are you saying?"

"If I could give them to you, I—"

"Hold it. I don't begrudge you for manifesting powers. If anything, it's better I didn't. I'm not the most patient man. I have a temper and I'm prone to tunnel vision."

My dad's mouth curved. "Tell us more."

Brian made a face. "I'm saying there's no one more suited to helping others than you. You're kind and compassionate. Patient enough to build your education, hone your skills."

"We're not a burden?"

"You're family. My family." He coughed, cheeks flushing. "In any case, I'm proud of you."

The praise startled me. "Yeah?"

"Took on a ring of kidnappers from what we heard." Brian scowled. "Though they haven't given us the details."

Footsteps in the hall. Jase stood in the doorway, holding a pale pink bakery box. He wore a deep grey shirt and jeans, looked casual.

And miserable. His hair was messy, his eyes shadowed. Dark bruises bloomed over his face, his knuckles. Butterfly bandages stretched across a gash on his cheekbone.

Seeing him injured made my heart clutch. It was part of the superhero deal. We risked everything, every time. Still, it was another reminder of how human he was. How vulnerable.

When my dad and uncle stared at me, I cleared my throat. "Dad, Uncle Brian, this is Jase Park. My project partner and boyfriend." The last word came out a little high pitched.

Brian straightened. "Oh?"

My dad chuckled, stepped around to shake hands. "I'm Briar's dad, Phil. Seems you saved my daughter's life."

"No. She's the one always saving me."

Brian started to speak when my dad clapped a hand on his shoulder. "Jase, how do you like your burgers?"

"Ah, medium. Loaded."

"Brian and I will pick some up. We'll talk when we get back." He gave me the most obvious wink in the world before steering his reluctant brother towards the door.

As they swept out of the room, I exhaled. My relationship with my uncle would probably always be strained. But he'd been there when I needed him and my dad loved us both.

For now, it was enough.

Jase sat on the stool next to my bed. "Sorry I wasn't here when you woke."

"I think you were. I was in and out for awhile and I swear I heard your voice telling me I was going to be okay." I glanced at the box, sniffed at the enticing aroma. "For me?"

"Cookies."

"Give me one while you debrief me."

He opened the lid, pulled out a chocolate chip. "You've been out for about a day," he said, breaking it in half and feeding it to me. "After the fight, Hector found on-campus security. They helped us secure the criminal PNs, get the captives out. The institute's running the investigation now."

"The others?"

"Some injuries, otherwise okay. Tristan took the worst of it. He's in recovery, but he's conscious. Linden's body is still unstable. Who knows what the long term effects of those experiments are."

I ate more cookies, letting Jase feed me at a measured pace. "And he was going to do the same to others." The idea pissed me off all over again. "What about the latents? Cassi."

"Cassi's okay. Mona and Ashley, too. They're here in the hospital." He turned somber. "One of the latents didn't make it. They'd been experimenting on him for awhile. Whatever's going on, there've been deaths."

I thought back to the creepy playroom. "Those kids."

"Alive. We'll have to wait and see if they develop abilities or suffer any side effects." He paused. "You set a trap without telling me."

"Serena said if I told anyone, they'd hurt Cassi. I didn't know what kind of abilities they had, I couldn't risk it. Plus I had to make it convincing." I bit my lip. "Did you think I'd betrayed you?"

"No. You were devastated when you put me under. Besides, you're a lousy liar. They had a secondary location on Osprey Beach Park. Linden has a beach rental there."

"That's why they used the area for kidnapping."

"All Linden had to do was talk about his research, promise them a way to manifest abilities. Though with my sister, he framed it as a meeting to discuss possible disciplinary actions against me."

He ate one of the cookies. "He bribed security to keep them away from the building, had one of the tech savvy crew generate the false messages. Thought of everything."

"We don't know who's behind this. Linden mentioned the Patron, though it's got to be a code name."

"The investigators might get something from Serena. She's got family on the outside, and it's her first criminal act. Landmine isn't talking, and her crew doesn't know anything."

He set the box aside. "Feeling better?"

"Much." I meant it. Obviously the hospital had given me enough fuel to replenish. I was groggy and shaky, wouldn't be able to use my ability for a few days, but between the treatment, the food, and the day's rest, I was on my way to recovering.

Jase propped his elbows on the bed, held my hand between his as he closed his eyes.

"Hey." I squeezed his hand, hoping to soothe. "I'm alright. It's okay."

"Hell it is." His voice came out choked. "You almost—" He paused, shook his head. "If you'd given any more, you might've gone torpid."

"It's my way of fighting. You give your all in the field. So do I."

He blew out a breath. "Next time, hold a little back. For my sake."

I pushed myself up. "I want to check on the others and sign myself out."

"You sure?"

"I'm tough. I have an official villain name now and everything." I grinned when he laughed. "And we have a project to finish."

43 STRONGHOLD

I smoothed a hand down the front of my tux. Beside me, Hector ate his way through a plate of fancy crackers covered with fancy cheese and paper-thin slices of fancy meat.

"Great speech," he said between bites. "I choked up."

"I'll give you something to choke on, Diaz."

An elbow nudged my ribs. I shot Briar a glare, but it turned into a smile. She was too pretty, her bridesmaid dress the color of deep red wine.

The city was a bright carpet of lights against the late December night. Iceberg's sprawling rooftop had been transformed, draped with gauzy white fabrics and floating fairy lights. Guests clustered at food stations or crowded the dance floor, laughing and talking. Outdoor heating lamps created a dome of warmth, keeping everyone toasty.

Vivid red and crisp white flowers filled clear glass vases. More bloomed along handrails decorated with winter greenery. Champagne and special cocktails stood in neat rows at drink stations, glittering in the overhanging lights. The air smelled of cool Florida winter and flowers. Music, cheerful conversations, and the click of heels on the dance floor created a rhythm of sound.

Cassi and Alba beamed at one another as they led the dancing. Both wore knee-length cream colored dresses and sparkling pins in their hair.

Hector tossed his plate onto a table, then blinked out. He appeared by a startled Hazel, spinning her onto the dance floor. Tristan stood alone by the roof's edge, looking out over the city.

My parents were near the drink station, both in formal wear. Likely with their bodysuits underneath. Though it was Christmas Eve, they were no doubt going straight from the celebrations to work. Still, having them there meant a lot to Cassi.

After the ceremony, my father had paused next to me, studied my face for a long moment. "Good work," he'd said before moving on. It was as high a compliment as I could've hoped for.

Now they stood speaking to Lucie. She nodded and replied, but sadness lingered in her eyes.

Briar's hand slipped into mine. I brought her hand to my mouth, pressed a kiss to her knuckles. "You look good."

She opened her fingers to touch my jaw. "So do you. Very proper gentleman."

"We both know that's a lie."

"I prefer former bad boys anyway." She sipped her champagne. "Glad the semester's over."

"Been a hell of a ride."

"Can't believe the board wants us to present our theses to the entire department." She scowled. "Now we have to make slides."

"The horror," I said, not meaning it. The extra work meant extending our partnership over winter break. Something I was looking forward to.

Dr. Singh was, too.

"We're talking an interdepartmental project. This is going to effect the institute for years to come," she'd said. "I'm going to video it and have it front and center on the institute's website."

"Great," I muttered. Next to me, Briar laughed.

"Are you two sure you don't need an extension? After what happened with Linden, we could easily request more time." She said her fellow professor's name with a note of bitterness. The knowledge of Linden's involvement had shocked everyone. The institute would be dealing with the ramifications for years.

"We can handle it," Briar said, meeting my eyes. "I want to end the semester clean."

"Then we'll make it happen," Dr. Singh said, fired up. "Let's take a look at templates."

Between that, the time it took us to heal, the on-going investigation, she and I hadn't had much time to talk. Wouldn't be much in the future either.

It'd taken weeks for everything to settle. The hospital wanted to keep everyone under observation. Tristan took the longest to recover. Apparently they'd been forced to operate on him while using limiters. Made me wonder what the hell kind of crazy ability the guy was harboring.

Dr. Linden remained under close observation, his body continuing to fluctuate. The institute took custody of him, the weird chamber, the kids. None of them seemed effected as of yet. The teens who'd manifested abilities had since lost them, their bodies returning to latent states.

Landmine was put under special arrest. This time with no chance of early release. Higher ups assured me the investigation would get their full attention.

I fisted my hands, wondered if even now, someone was kidnapping more latents. Was it because they shared Linden's vision of creating more PNs, or did they have a more insidious agenda?

Another nudge to my ribs. "This is a wedding. You're supposed to get drunk and listen to embarrassing stories."

"The only thing embarrassing here is Diaz's dance."

"They're cute. He's gone on her. Can't you tell?"

I tried to see it. Failed. "We have our own relationship to worry about."

"You're worried?"

"You are. You're worried I haven't mentioned what you said. You think I'm going to push you away?"

She hugged one of her arms across her middle. "Maybe I could've chosen a better time and place."

"You're wrong. It was the perfect time and place. Because it was you."

"You mean it?"

I did. The Powerhouse life wasn't easy. There were no guarantees, no safe routes.

But I wanted to spend every moment of it by her side.

I cupped her face in my palms. "I want to be in your life. Want you to be in mine. I love you, Briar."

The words tumbled out, reckless and unplanned. The tight grip I'd kept on myself was gone, shredded to nothing in front of her.

Her eyes filled, her fingers clutching the front of my jacket. "I love you, Jase."

I let the fierce wave of emotion crash through me. "Tell me what you want and I'll give it to you."

"All I want is us. The way we are. No bargains, no ultimatums. Just us." Her brows lifted. "Unless you think I should ditch my sloth pajamas."

"I wouldn't change one thing about you."

"Same here. And whatever comes, we'll handle it." Her fingers laced through mine. "Together."

She leaned into me, stretching onto her toes for a kiss. Her laugh changed into a yelp as I caught her up. Crushing her to my chest, I spun in circles. She flung her arms around my neck, holding me tight. In the background, I heard voices egging us on.

"My place," I said, still holding her. "After we get out of here."

"For midnight snacks?"

"And sex. Lots of sex."

She smiled as I leaned in for another kiss. "It's a deal."

AFTERWORD

Thank you for reading STUNNER, the first book in the POWERHOUSE INSTITUTE series! It makes my geek girl heart happy to have it out in the world and in the hands of readers.

Special thanks to writer pals Moni and Reghan for their support and encouragement, and to Elizabeth Briggs for all her advice and guidance.

Help me grow as an author by leaving a review, it helps readers like you find my books. Don't forget to join the newsletter fam for news, exclusive peeks, and free reads!

RUSH JOB - EXCERPT

Ready for more? Read on for the first chapter of RUSH JOB, a POWERHOUSE INSTITUTE novella!

RUSH

Most college students spend summer term road tripping, studying abroad, partying on the beach.

Being broke, I opted for a part-time job.

I held the trespasser at arm's length, avoiding his attempts to slap, kick, and bite me. "Sir, if you don't have a pass, I'm afraid you'll have to leave."

"Let me in, man! I gotta meet him, man!"

"Sorry, man. No can do."

"You're a bitch, man!" He kicked, legs flailing. His pupils were enormous. Why someone would get high and decide crashing their fave celeb's hotel is a good idea was beyond me.

While he foamed, I straightened, my long hair swinging

from the high ponytail I'd tied. On a whim, I'd dyed it pale blonde. Other than that, I resembled my Asian-American dad. Straight hair, gold skin, dark eyes.

My temper? All from my mom

Shrieking, the trespasser flung himself headlong at me.

My ability flared to life, increasing my speed to far beyond normal. In a blink, I raced to the exit door, propped it open with the bar, raced back just in time to stick out my leg.

The trespasser tripped, stumbled right out the door.

I closed it behind him, returned to my station. The narrow corridor I'd been assigned lead to one of the side entrances, which made it a prime spot for fans trying to sneak in. I'd already tracked and disposed of two camdrones spying on the building.

"Nice work."

I turned. A man stood at the end of the hallway, wearing a black suit and white shirt similar to mine. Though judging by his "Security Detail" badge, he was one of the official staff working for the charge. I was extra muscle, hired by the hotel.

"Thanks," I said, glancing at his name badge. It read "Nate Strigidae."

"Nate, I'm Reina Tan."

We both lingered over the handshake. Nate had a grown up boy next door hotness that had my senses humming. His fingertips bore rough calluses, making me wonder if he played guitar.

"Nice gloves."

I looked at my fingerless fighter's gloves, bright pink over black. "Thanks."

I studied him for a moment. "Are you a PN?"

"Normal."

Surprising. Most security firms sprung for PNs. I wondered if the guy was a martial arts master or a tech expert.

"You know the charge?" he asked.

"Rich guy, I guess." I'd skimmed the files, memorized the photos. Apparently he was being escorted to an important meeting.

Didn't matter, as I'd never be in the same room with him. I was getting paid to guard a specific hallway during specific times.

"You look kind of like him," I said.

"One of the reasons they hired me."

Body doubles. Not uncommon.

"I'm surprised you didn't mistake me for him," Nate said.

"You're a good two inches taller. Your nose and cheekbones are sharper." I tapped my finger under my bottom lip. "You've got a small mole here and your incisor is slightly crooked."

"You're good."

"Part of the gig, paying attention to faces."

"You've got a great face."

"Bold."

"Is it a turn off?"

I studied him for a moment. Tall and lean, skin pale against his black suit. His hair gleamed a rich, chestnut brown, contrasting vivid blue eyes. A lapel pin in the shape of a stylized owl rested on his collar. A thick, matte metal ring, the surface etched with a striking design, encircled his left thumb.

I decided a little flirting wouldn't hurt. If it lead to more, that wouldn't hurt either.

What the hell. It was my final summer before becoming an official Powerhouse. My last chance to live it up.

I gave him my best sultry smile. "Not yet."

"Buy you a drink?"

An hour later, we were sinking pool balls and nursing frothy beers.

The small pub was one of many in Mayport's downtown

scene. This one, "Whitby's," leaned British. Dark wood furniture, patterned upholstery, and signs boasting authentic ale.

No idea how authentic the ale was, but it was damn delicious.

Servers hurried past, carrying heavy wooden trays loaded with drinks and pub food. Bots bused empty tables, robotic arms clicking and grasping. A real wood fire snapped and flickered in the fireplace, despite the fact it was Florida in May. The air smelled of alcohol and bar snacks.

"Five, corner," I called, lining up my shot. Balls clacked, the white one spinning against the field as the bright orange sank clean.

"You're going to run the table at this rate," Nate said.

"Not your lucky night."

"I think it is." His attention lingered on my ass as I bent over.

Smirking, I purposely stretched out the pose before studying the next shot. "Six, side."

We'd both removed our blazers, leaving them slung over a coat tree. Nate pushed up his sleeves, showing off lean forearms. Made me wonder what the rest of him looked like.

I missed, took the opportunity to devour a double serving of fish and chips. Part of being a PN, using my ability left me ravenous. Especially speedsters, we're constantly hungry.

Plus it gave me the chance to admire his ass while he took his shot.

"What do you do when you're not hired muscle?" he asked.

"I'm getting into the institute this year. It's about damn time, too."

"Yeah?"

"You have to be twenty-one or older, so I did two years of state after high school." Pretty common for those hoping for

Powerhouse status. Still, the extra years chafed me. I wanted to get in, get out, and get on with my life.

"You?" I asked.

"Software."

A tech expert, then. "Moonlighting?"

"I'm a man of many interests."

"What are you interested in tonight?"

His gaze flicked up from the table, locked on mine as he sank the six. "Getting past security."

I smirked, finished my beer, looking forward to the night ahead.

One night turned into a week turned into a month. I'd wrap up my shift and Nate would be waiting for me in the security room. We'd hit up a bar for drinks, food, games. A few times we changed it up. Caught the latest summer blockbuster before hitting up a food truck.

Each night we spent together had me liking Nate more and more. He was on the quiet side, but he kept pace with my competitive streak, beyond plus for me. Men sometimes found me intimidating, however Nate took my outrageous table calls and increasingly daring challenges in stride.

He loved music. I'd catch him tapping his fingers to whatever played through the bar speakers. He was a living music recognition app, instantly recognizing songs and knowing the artist and history, even from remixes or covers.

Occasionally he'd pull up an HC screen and make quick notes to himself. Strange little floating bubbles, sharp marks and dots.

"An alien language?" I asked once.

"Musical notation." He rubbed the back of his head. "Sort of. I taught myself so it's bastardized. Mixed with mathematical notation."

Whoa, taught himself? Meanwhile, I'd almost gotten in a fight with the bathroom soap dispenser.

He nodded at my gloves. "You wear those all the time?"

"Yup." I flexed my fists, the worn, cared for leather giving a satisfying creak. "My dad gave me my first pair when I was a kid. Left them on my bed with a note, 'For the girl with the bright pink hair.'"

"Pink hair, huh?" Nate studied me as if trying to imagine it.

I grinned. "When I confronted him, he'd claimed they'd been left mysteriously on the doorstep like an orphan child in fairy tales. He's always pulling Santa Claus acts."

"Nice guy."

"And patient. Got to be to put up with me for a daughter."

Nate laughed, and I got a glimpse of his crooked incisor. The sight of it made me imagine kissing him. Touching him. Being touched by those calloused fingers. Each day that passed, I found myself liking him more and more.

So why the hell hadn't he made a move?

There'd been plenty of heated looks and suggestions. He'd skim his hand down my arm and I'd trail a finger over the collar of his blazer. I'd given him the subtle "come in for a cup of coffee" line and the straight up obvious "my place is around the corner."

No bite.

A few times he'd start to say something, then stop. His brows would draw together and a tight expression would cross his features. A second later, he'd be back to his quiet, contemplative self.

By the time June rolled around, I was ready to skip the foreplay and shove him onto the pool table.

I jiggled my leg, tapping my heel against the floor. Had I read the signs wrong? Maybe he wasn't interested in me or in women or in sex. Nothing wrong with any of that. But I needed to know.

It was time to ask outright. There were only a few days left on the job. If Nate was part of the charge's permanent security detail, he'd be gone with them.

My chest tightened. I'd miss him. Despite the sexual tension, we'd become friends, able to laugh, talk, hang out. Weird, since I'd first imagined him as a one night.

"Good game," he said, dismissing the table. The pool set up disappeared, the holotable reverting to its blank slate and scrolling menu of game options.

"Beers on me?" I asked.

"I want to be sober." He met my eyes. "For tonight."

My pulse kicked. "I hope you don't mean another round of pool."

"I mean a round with you, whirlwind. In bed. Naked and under me."

Hell, yes, I thought.

Out loud, I said, "Maybe you'll be the one under me."

"Even better." He grabbed my jacket, helped me into it.

As I slipped my arms through the sleeves, he rested his hands on my shoulders. His head lowered, bringing his mouth close to my ear. "My hotel's close."

His breath blew across my skin, the low spoken words vibrating through me. I shivered, caught the scent of his shaving cream.

"Well, then," I said. "What are we waiting for?"

Want more superpowered romance? Head to my website athenafranco.com to check out the rest of the POWERHOUSE INSTITUTE series!

ALSO BY ATHENA FRANCO

THE POWERHOUSE INSTITUTE Series

RUSH JOB

STUNNER

HECTIC

KNIGHTFALL

Find all of these and more on my website:

athenafranco.com

ABOUT THE AUTHOR

Athena Franco is an author of fantastical romances with inclusive casts, high heat, and intense action. With a Bachelor's in Psychology and a Master's in Public Health, she spent years working in the non-profit arena before returning to her one true love: telling stories.

She's traveled much of the world and, as a Navy wife, has lived all over the U.S. When not writing, she can be found playing video games or spoiling her dog.

You can follow Athena on her Amazon author page and across social media.

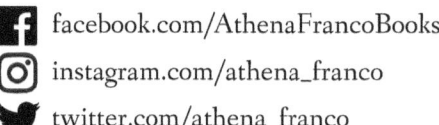

facebook.com/AthenaFrancoBooks
instagram.com/athena_franco
twitter.com/athena_franco